M000190916

THE WIZARD OF OZ

WHERE IS HE NOW?

THE WIZARD OF OZ

WHERE IS HE NOW?

RICHARD MICKELSON

The Wizard of Oz
Where Is He Now?

Written by Richard Mickelson
Illustrated by Patty Fleckenstein

TATE PUBLISHING
AND ENTERPRISES, LLC

Published by Tate Publishing & Enterprises, LLC
127 E. Trade Center Terrace | Mustang, Oklahoma 73064 USA
1.888.361.9473 | www.tatepublishing.com

Tate Publishing is committed to excellence in the publishing industry. The company reflects the philosophy established by the founders, based on Psalm 68:11,
"The Lord gave the word and great was the company of those who published it."

Book design copyright © 2014 by Tate Publishing, LLC. All rights reserved.
Cover design by Joel Uber
Interior design by Jomel Pepito

Published in the United States of America

ISBN: 978-1-63449-153-2
1. Fiction / General
2. Fiction / Fairy Tales, Folk Tales, Legends & Mythology
14.08.01

DEDICATION

This book is dedicated to my wife Paula my favorite wizard. Without her urging and guidance, this story would have never been told.

TABLE OF CONTENTS

CHAPTER I

WHY ME?

Rosebud was madder than she had ever been in her life. With fists clenched, she raced up the sidewalk toward home. Fire was in her emerald eyes. A dark blue backpack slapped furiously against her tiny waist. One of her long, red braids had been unraveled and was as frizzy as a squirrel's tail. Rosebud screamed in dismay when she looked at her clothes. Her favorite blue plaid shirt and dungarees were torn and dirty. This was the result of yet another fight in the schoolyard with some of her cruel, uncaring fellow students, a fight that had started because of her tiny size.

You see, Rosebud was a short Munchkin, standing only seventeen inches tall. She was a senior at Munchkin High School, yet she was only half the size of the kids in the lower grades. This bothered her terribly, and she longed to be taller.

Every day after school, four or five of the school bullies would wait for Rosebud. Like all bullies, they loved to pick on smaller kids. When Rosebud came into view, they would shout insults. "Runt, short stuff, shrimp, peewee," and other hurting names rolled off their snarling lips. Rosebud would ignore them, but when she attempted to walk away, they would jump out, block the sidewalk, and taunt her some more. This made her furious, and though she knew there was no winning, Rosebud would attack. The bullies would pull her backpack off and throw it aside. Then they would grab Rosebud and toss her back and forth like a sack of flour. When they tired of playing toss, they would roll her on the ground like a ball. After they were done having their fun, they would hang her backpack backwards, around the front of her neck, and undo one of her braids. Rosebud would run away from the bullies with tears in her eyes. "Look at the half-pint run," they would shout. Rosebud could hear them taunting and laughing as she pulled off her backpack and slung it over her shoulders. How humiliating!

She rounded the corner and ran up the street toward home. A stone the size of a golf ball lay in front of her on the sidewalk. Without thinking, she decided to take out her frustrations on it.

An enraged Rosebud screamed, "Someday you bullies will be sorry for what you've done to me!" With that, she kicked the large stone so hard that it flew across the street and struck the curb with a loud bang. "Yeow!" Rosebud howled in pain, hopping down the street and holding on tightly to her injured right toe. "What else can go wrong today? Can't anything go right?" she shouted.

Rosebud hopped up the porch steps on one foot and banged open the front door. She started wailing, "Why me, Mama?" and slammed the door shut with such force that it practically flew off of its hinges. Then she whipped the backpack off of her shoulders, grabbed it by a strap with both hands, spun around twice, and let it fly. The backpack came open as it flew like a rocket, dumping its contents, scattering books, homework, and leftover lunch from one end of the hallway to the other. Rosebud plopped down in the middle of the mess sobbing pitifully. "Everybody hates me because I'm so small," she cried.

Rosebud's mother, Mama Bellpepper, was in the kitchen making one of her delicious apple pies for dessert. The slamming door startled her, and she almost jumped out of her shoes.

"Rosebud, is that you? Are you okay?" Mama shouted. Mama wiped the cinnamon, flour, and sugar off of her hands onto her bright red apron as she ran from the kitchen.

Mama Bellpepper was a typical Munchkin wife and mother. She stood a little less than four feet tall and wore a pink, flowery, full-length dress. A matching red bandana was wrapped around her striking salt and pepper hair. On her legs and feet were knee-length, red woolen stockings and black, curly-toed shoes with shiny silver buckles.

What in the world can I do about this problem? Mama Bellpepper thought. Mama knew that her teenage daughter was undersized, and that this made Rosebud the target of countless cruel taunts and snide remarks from the school bullies. The problem would not be easy to resolve unless someone could find a way to make Rosebud taller. But how do you make someone taller? And what kind of a person could do it?

Rosebud's yellow cat, Apricot, was licking the spattered, leftover lunch off the floor and the wall. Like Rosebud, Apricot was very small. Though fully grown, Apricot was no bigger than a chipmunk, and had gotten the name because of her apricot-colored fur.

Mama sat down next to Rosebud and put an arm around her. "It's the same thing again, isn't it, child?"

The sweet smell of cinnamon and apples on her mother's warm hands, hands that calmly stroked her red hair in a soothing manner, made Rosebud feel better.

Rosebud turned to Mama with tear-swollen eyes and a dripping nose. In a whimpering voice, she said, "Yes, it's the same thing, Mama, and I'm really sick of it. Look at my new dungarees and blue plaid shirt. They're torn and dirty and ruined! See how they unraveled my braid!"

Rosebud snuggled close and sobbed into her mother's warm chest.

"Go ahead and cry, Rosebud. It will do you good."

"Why can't I be tall like the other kids? I just want to crawl into a hole and die."

Mama tenderly wiped Rosebud's tears away with the flap of her apron. The white flour from the apron made Rosebud's face look as pale as a ghost's.

"God has put each of us here for a purpose. You'll find yours. Don't forget about—"

But before Mama could finish, Rosebud interrupted, saying, "Please, Mama, don't talk to me about famous short Munchkins. I've heard it all before. It doesn't change anything. I've got to find a way to become taller. But how?"

"I know, child. I'm trying. Don't let those bullies ruin your life."

"My life is already ruined. No one wants to take me to the prom, and I almost fall over every time I put my backpack on. Besides, no one would ever want to marry someone my size." Rosebud moaned.

"Don't be too sure about that, child. A short boy Munchkin is out there someplace who is having the same problems. What we need to do is find him."

"And if there isn't? Then what, Mama?"

"Well, child…" Mama said as she gazed into Rosebud's sad, tear-swollen eyes. "I guess I don't know then what."

Mama Bellpepper also had a broken heart, for she knew not what to do for her tiny child. They sat there for a long time hugging and crying softly on each other's shoulder. Then a wry smile appeared on Mama's face.

"I've got it!" Mama whispered in Rosebud's ear.

The startled Rosebud whispered back, "Got what, Mama?"

"The answer to your problem!"

"What is it? Please tell me right away. What is it?"

Mama Bellpepper rose to her feet and gleefully announced. "The answer is—the Wizard of Oz! After all, child, wasn't it he who helped the Tin Man get a heart and the Scarecrow a brain?"

"Yes, he did, Mama. And don't forget that the Wizard of Oz helped the Cowardly Lion to be courageous too," Rosebud said, jumping to her feet and strutting like the cowardly lion.

"There's absolutely no reason why the Wizard of Oz couldn't help you to become taller?" Mama said. "Come on, child, let's go ask him."

"You're wonderful, Mama! Why didn't you think of it sooner?" Rosebud gave her a big hug and a sloppy kiss.

"I don't know why I didn't think of it sooner. But I've thought of it now, and we're off to see the Wizard, the wonderful Wizard of Oz. And if all goes well, when we return home, you'll be a lot taller."

The two of them grabbed their bonnets and headed for the front door. Rosebud stopped at the hall mirror to wipe away her tears. When she saw that her face and hair were covered with flour and that flowing tears had made weird streams down both of her cheeks, she and Mama began to laugh and laugh.

"I have a feeling that something wonderful is going to happen to me today," Rosebud said, sticking out her tongue and waving goodbye to the mirror.

"I agree," said Mama sticking out her tongue, too.

At last there was hope. Rosebud continued to laugh delightedly. She picked up Apricot, gave her a hug and a kiss, and put her in the empty backpack. Then she and Mama bounced out the front door, holding hands and dancing in a circle.

They skipped merrily down the yellow brick road toward the Emerald City and the wonderful Wizard of Oz. "I know that the Wizard of Oz is about to fulfill my lifelong dream, Mama. I'll soon be as tall, or taller, than the other Munchkin children. I might even be taller than you. Won't that be wonderful?" Rosebud did two cartwheels and a flip.

"Yes, it will, Rosebud. Yes, it will," Mama said, wringing her hands. *What if he can't make her taller? Then what?*

CHAPTER II

ANOTHER WAY TO GROW TALLER

Rosebud and Mama were halfway to the Emerald City when they came upon Dorothy and her dog, Toto. Dorothy was picking wild gooseberries, and Toto was having fun chasing squirrels.

Apricot heard Toto barking and stuck her head out of the backpack to see what he was so excited about. Toto spotted Apricot and began to bark louder, hoping she would join him in this fun game of chase.

"Hush, Toto!" Dorothy said, turning to greet Rosebud and Mama.

Dorothy gave them a polite, little curtsy. "Good afternoon, Mama Bellpepper and Rosebud. How are you today?"

"And a good afternoon to you too, Dorothy," said Rosebud.

"We couldn't be better!" said Mama as the two of them returned the polite curtsy.

"Where are you going?" Dorothy asked, offering them a handful of fresh-picked wild gooseberries.

"No, thank you," said Rosebud. "Mama and I are going to the Emerald City to ask the Wizard of Oz to make me taller."

Dorothy beamed at them. "That will be wonderful. If the Wizard of Oz can't make you taller, you can accompany the two of us to Kansas in the morning. I know that you'll grow taller there, because I'll feed you lots of delicious Kansas corn. It makes everyone grow tall."

"I'll have some wild gooseberries," said Mama, holding out her hands. "How are you and the Wizard of Oz getting to Kansas?" a worried Mama asked.

"The Wizard of Oz and I are planning to take a balloon ride to Kansas. Rosebud should ask him if she could fly with us. There's plenty of room in our basket for someone her size. And when Rosebud grows taller, I'll send her home. What do you think of that idea?"

Rosebud was shaking with excitement and replied, "I think it's a wonderful idea, for now I have two options, either the Wizard of Oz making me taller, or flying with him in a balloon to Kansas."

Mama was nervously clenching her hands. "Where is Kansas?" she asked. "Is it safe? How will you send Rosebud back home after she grows tall?"

Dorothy thought a moment, then replied, "I don't know where Kansas is from here, nor does the Wizard of Oz, but we're going up in the big balloon tomorrow in the hopes of finding it. I do know that Rosebud will be safe in Kansas, since she can stay on the farm with Auntie Em, Uncle Henry, and me. However, I have no idea how Rosebud will get back home again. Perhaps the Wizard of Oz can bring her when he returns to the Emerald City."

"I don't like the idea, Dorothy. There's too much risk." Mama was getting edgy. "What if you could never return home to us, Rosebud?"

Dorothy held Mama Bellpepper's hand and said, "There's risk in everything we do, Mama. If you don't take a chance now and then, you may never get where you want to be in life. I want to go home so badly that I'm willing to do almost anything to get there. I have no guarantees from the Wizard of Oz that we'll make it to Kansas, but I believe we will, and so does he. I promise you this, Mama Bellpepper, I'll take good care of Rosebud on our trip and watch over her when we get to Kansas, but that's the best that I can do."

"That's the way I feel too, Mama, and I'm ready to take a chance and fly to Kansas. Can I please go, Mama?" Rosebud begged.

"Okay, Rosebud! Just go do it!" Mama replied.

Mama and Rosebud said goodbye to Dorothy and continued down the yellow brick road, singing and dancing as they went on their merry way.

Dorothy shouted, "Don't the two of you worry about flying to Kansas. I have no doubt that the Wizard of Oz will make you taller today. Don't you think so, too?"

Rosebud wondered, *Can the Wizard of Oz really make me taller? Or will I have to take the perilous, unknown flight to a place called Kansas?*

CHAPTER III

A VERY
BUSY WIZARD

Mama and Rosebud arrived at Emerald City and knocked on the large green gate for admission. A small green door slid open, and a little green man with a gruff voice stuck his head out of the opening and shouted, "If you want to gain entry to Emerald City, you must pull the lime green ribbon hanging to the left of this gate."

The little green man slid the door shut with a rather loud bang.

Rosebud was jumping in the air. "I see the ribbon, "but I can't reach it."

"I'll get it!" Mama grabbed the ribbon and gave it a mighty tug. The bell rang long and loud.

The small door slid open once again, and the little green man screeched, "What are you trying to do, break my eardrums? Now pull the ribbon again, and this time," the little green man whispered, "pull it so the bell rings softly." .

"He sounds rather upset," said Mama, barely tugging on the ribbon. The bell pealed softly.

The small door slid open, and the little green man demanded to know, "What are you doing here? State your business. I haven't got all day."

"Why…why… we're here to see the great Wizard of Oz," Rosebud said. Apricot warily watched the little green man from the safety of the backpack.

"Well, why didn't you say so?" the little green man replied with a smile. "Why have you been standing outside all this time? Come in, come in."

The gate swung open to allow them entry. Apricot hissed at the little green man as they entered the gate, and the little green man hissed back.

The funny-looking, little green man was dressed in a green uniform. He was wearing a green tall hat, green shoes, and one green glove on his right hand, the same hand he used to open and close the large green gate and the little green door. He demanded, "What do you want?"

"We came to ask the Wizard of Oz to make Rosebud taller," Mama Bellpepper told him.

"She seems tall enough to me. Wait here and don't move," the little green man said.

He then turned his back to them, and just as quickly, turned around to face them again.

"Since you are still here, you must all wear green glasses while you're in Emerald City or you'll be arrested, and so will your funny-looking, little cat. It's my duty to lock the glasses onto your eyes. It's also my duty to unlock and remove the glasses when you leave." He then took three pairs of green glasses from a green box and locked them onto their eyes.

"How wonderfully green everything looks." Rosebud smiled.

Mama Bellpepper was amazed, "I've never seen grass so green," she said.

"The Wizard of Oz is in the big green castle right beyond the City Square. Now be on your way, aaannnd—Goood luuuccck!" the little green man said with a funny grin.

"What does he mean by good luck, Mama?"

"I have no idea, Rosebud. But I'm sure we'll soon find out."

Mama and Rosebud were hurrying to the castle when they noticed that a large crowd had gathered in the City Square. The two of them moved cautiously into the crowd and stood next to a girl wearing a green dress, green shoes, and green earrings. "Why is this crowd here?" Mama asked the girl.

The little girl gave them a curtsy and a smile. "The Wizard of Oz is readying his balloon to take Dorothy and Toto back to Kansas tomorrow," she said. "We're here to help him prepare for his journey."

"Rosebud, get on my shoulders. We're going to the front of this crowd to see the Wizard of Oz, and I don't want you to be stepped on." With that, Mama pushed her way to the front of the crowd. Rosebud and Mama were awestruck, for before them stood the great Wizard of Oz. He was a rather portly man with a round face, short white hair, and a short white beard. On the ground in front of him lay a big, brightly colored balloon with various shades of green silk.

Mama asked a helper, "Why is the balloon lying on the ground?"

"We placed the balloon in a neat circle so it could be easily filled with hot air in the morning."

"What are the ropes and laundry basket for?" Mama asked.

"We use the heavy ropes to attach the basket to the balloon. We hope that the ropes are strong enough so that they don't break and dump everyone out when the balloon takes off."

"Why doesn't the Wizard of Oz take some of the food and clothes out of the basket and lighten the load?" Rosebud asked.

"He has to have enough supplies to last a week. And who knows what the weather will be?" he said.

After placing everything on board, the Wizard of Oz realized that there was barely enough room for him and Dorothy. The basket was so crammed full that Dorothy would have to sit on the pile of clothing and hold Toto on her lap. He was wondering to himself, *Can this balloon get off the ground with this much weight in it?*

The Wizard of Oz was reading over his last-minute checklist to make sure everything was prepared for the journey. He did not see Rosebud slip off of Mama's shoulders and approach him.

Rosebud was trembling like a lone leaf on an oak tree in the middle of winter. She couldn't believe that she was in the presence of one so powerful. Rosebud spoke fearfully in a high-strung, squeaky voice. "Hello, great Wizard of Oz."

The Wizard of Oz turned to see who was talking to him and didn't notice tiny Rosebud standing at his feet. He was rather upset to see Mama Bellpepper facing him, since he was very busy and didn't have time for anyone.

"What do you want?" he asked Mama, almost tripping over Rosebud. "Sorry, child, I didn't see you down there. My, you certainly are a tiny one."

This brought a roar of laughter from the crowd.

"Oh great wizard, being tiny is what I want to talk to you about."

"Shoo, child. I'm busy and have no time for you right now," the annoyed Wizard said.

Rosebud was angry that the Wizard of Oz had almost tripped over her and was shooing her away. She faced him boldly, put her hands on her hips, and said, "Oh wonderful Wizard of Oz, I'm so tiny that people are constantly tripping over me like you almost did. It's very embarrassing when this happens, and everyone laughs like the crowd around you was doing. Some of the kids at my school are always making fun of me, and bullying me because of my size. I only want to be taller like everyone else, so I can get even with them. It's said that you are a great Wizard and can make me taller. Please do it!" Rosebud pleaded, gasping for breath after her tirade. Apricot and Mama Bellpepper were staring wide-eyed in disbelief at Rosebud's courage.

"First of all, child, I will not do anything for anyone who is out for revenge," the Wizard of Oz warned.

"I just want to get even for the terrible things they have done to me," Rosebud replied, regretting that she had said such a thing.

"Do you think that the people who are mean and pick on you are equal to or lower than you?" asked the Wizard of Oz.

"They're certainly lower than I am!" Rosebud said.

"Then why would you want to lower yourself to their level? Because that's what you will do when you try to get *even*. And don't forget it."

"I never thought of it that way, and I promise that I'll never try to get even with anybody. Now can you make me taller? Please?" she cried.

No one, including the townspeople, had any idea that the great Wizard of Oz was not a true wizard. There was no way he could grant a wish for Rosebud or anyone else. They didn't know he was using the balloon and Dorothy as a way to get out of Emerald City before it was discovered that he had no wizardly powers. He had to act fast, so he said in a menacing voice, "No, no, no! Not a chance, child! I'm very busy, and I don't have time to work my wizardry for you right now. So please get out of my way and be gone. I have much to do before my flight tomorrow, and I have no more time to talk to you."

"Why are you shooing Rosebud away?" asked Mama Bellpepper. "She's in desperate need of your help. It's said that you are a great wizard and that you can make my child taller. Why won't you do it now, and then we'll go home?"

"We wizards can only grant one wish at a time, and at this moment I'm working on Dorothy's. I can't possibly make Rosebud taller today. However, I do promise that I will use my magic and make her taller upon my return."

The Wizard of Oz made this promise with his fingers crossed behind his back.

"Why don't you please get along and stop bothering me!" he insisted.

"Suppose you don't return, oh great Wizard of Oz," Rosebud said. "Since you can't work your magic for me at this time, I have another idea. Dorothy told me to ask if I could ride with you on your journey to Kansas. If I can get to Kansas, she will feed me corn and I will grow taller. Please can I go with you, please?" she pleaded.

"Well, child, I would be happy to have you ride with us, but there isn't enough room in this basket for one more person, not even one as small as you."

Rosebud was not about to give up. "I can sit on Dorothy's lap. I don't eat much, and I won't be in the way. I promise."

Apricot ducked into the backpack as the Wizard of Oz picked up Rosebud and held her over the basket. "Look inside this basket. It's crammed full. In fact, it's so full and heavy that Dorothy may have to throw Toto out so we can get off the ground tomorrow. You, child, could be the straw that breaks the camel's back. In other words, even your little bit of weight could prevent us from rising into the air. Now please move along and let me get my work done."

"If we can't get off the ground, then I'll jump out," Rosebud said.

Mama put her hand over Rosebud's mouth and whispered in her ear, "No matter what you say, the Wizard of Oz will have an answer for you, and not one you want to hear. On our way home, we'll discuss some other things you can do to make yourself grow taller."

They left the Wizard of Oz and walked slowly toward the large green gate. Rosebud wept quietly while they walked. Mama put her arm around Rosebud and assured her that everything would be okay. They stopped briefly, while the little green man unlocked their green glasses and returned them to the green chest.

Noticing the tears in Rosebud's eyes, the little green man said, "Now you know why I wished you good luck. What are you going to do now?"

"I wish we knew," Mama said, wiping the tears from her eyes.

Mama Bellpepper and Rosebud were crying while they walked down the yellow brick road toward home. They had been so excited to see the Wizard of Oz, and now their dreams were shattered.

They hadn't gone very far when they came upon Dorothy and Toto, who were returning from picking wild gooseberries.

"Why are the two of you crying?" Dorothy asked.

Rosebud sobbed. "The Wizard of Oz has refused to work his magic and make me taller, and he also refused to let me ride with you in the balloon to Kansas. He said that the basket is too overloaded for me to come along."

"I can't believe that someone as tiny as you would overload the balloon. I have no doubt that after I talk to the Wizard of Oz, I'll convince him to let you come with us," Dorothy assured them.

"Oh, please do!" Rosebud begged.

"Let's see," Dorothy said, checking her watch. "It's six o'clock. You go home and pack for the trip, and I'll go talk to the Wizard of Oz. I'll meet you outside the large green gate at nine thirty tonight."

"What if the Wizard of Oz says no to you, too?" Mama called out to Dorothy.

"We'll cross that bridge when we come to it, but I don't believe that he'll say no to me," she said, giving them a confident smile and a thumbs-up.

Rosebud was once again filled with excitement and jumping into the air. "Let's go pack, Mama. Kansas, here I come!" she screamed.

Rosebud and Mama dashed into the house and began packing some clothing and food for the trip. Rosebud's daddy, Papa Parsleysprig, came home from work after they had finished packing.

Papa Parsleysprig was an accountant by trade and quite unusual for a Munchkin, because he was tall and thin, instead of short and squat. Papa, true to his trade, always wore a black suit, a white shirt, and a silk bow tie. He was never seen without several, number-two, yellow pencils with pink erasers sticking out of his suit pocket. Papa wore round, gold-rimmed glasses on the end of his nose and black, highly polished, curly-toed shoes with silver buckles.

Seeing the suitcase and bag of groceries in the hallway, Papa asked, "Is someone going on a trip?"

Mama Bellpepper explained to Papa Parsleysprig what had happened at their meeting with the Wizard of Oz and their conversation with Dorothy. "We're going to meet Dorothy at nine thirty tonight. She has promised that she will convince the Wizard of Oz to fly Rosebud to Kansas with them."

"What if the Wizard of Oz says no to Dorothy?" Papa asked.

"Dorothy has assured us that the Wizard of Oz won't say no to her."

"Won't it be wonderful, Papa? At last I'll be as tall as the other Munchkins," Rosebud cried with joy.

"It sure will be wonderful, my tiny Rosebud," Papa agreed.

Rosebud picked up Apricot to place her in the backpack, as the three of them prepared to depart for the Emerald City.

"I'm sorry, Rosebud, but you can't take Apricot with you," Mama said. If the Wizard of Oz thought that someone as tiny as you would overload the balloon, what do you think he'll say if you show up with your cat and cat food? You'll be home soon, and we'll take good care of Apricot while you're away," Mama promised.

"Your mother is right, Rosebud," said Papa. "Now say goodbye to Apricot, and let's be on our way."

Rosebud petted Apricot, gave her a hug, and put her inside the house. She would sorely miss her faithful companion. Apricot was meowing pitifully at the window, so Rosebud blew her a goodbye kiss, knowing she might never see her again. The three of them danced down the yellow brick road toward Emerald City and their meeting with Dorothy.

CHAPTER IV

MORE BAD NEWS

They arrived at the large green gate early and waited anxiously for Dorothy. At nine thirty, Dorothy showed up and immediately informed them that the Wizard of Oz had refused to take Rosebud on the trip to Kansas. "'We're way overloaded now,' he told me. I argued with him, but he remained steadfast in his refusal. I offered to leave some of my clothing behind, and he said, 'No! Rosebud can't go! You'll need all of your clothes for the trip.' No matter what I said, the Wizard of Oz found a reason to say no.

"Let's go home," said Papa. "There's nothing more we can do."

"Wait," said Dorothy. "I have another plan to get Rosebud to Kansas."

"What kind of plan?" Mama asked.

"I'm going to hide Rosebud on the basket tonight while it's dark."

"You mean she will be a stowaway. What if it doesn't work?" Papa asked.

"Yes, she will be a stowaway. I know it'll work, and once we get into the air, we can't land the balloon until it runs out of hot air. By that time, we'll be in Kansas. What do you say?"

"Okay. Let's do it!" said Mama.

"I noticed when I came to meet you that the guardian of the gate was fast asleep," Dorothy said. "This means that we won't have green glasses affixed to our eyes. When we sneak into Emerald City, we'll have to be very careful because if we're caught without them, we'll be arrested, and neither Rosebud nor I will make the trip to Kansas in the morning." Dorothy bent low and slipped through the gate. "Follow me, keep to the shadows, and whatever you do, don't wake the guardian."

Papa, Mama, and Rosebud bent low and followed Dorothy.

Fortunately, the guardian was a sound sleeper. No one noticed them, and no alarms were sounded.

The four of them arrived at the City Square and hid inside the green gazebo, staring at the basket, which to Rosebud seemed to be a mile away.

"Papa, you stay in this gazebo and keep an eye out for anyone coming this way," Dorothy whispered. "We three have to make it from here to the basket without being seen or we'll be arrested. If anyone approaches, you must keep them occupied and not let them see us, or all will be lost,"

"Don't worry, Dorothy, no one will get past me," Papa said confidently. "Now hurry and hide Rosebud in the basket before someone finds us and sounds the alarm."

Papa gave Rosebud a big hug and a kiss. "Everything will be fine, and we'll be together again soon," he promised.

"Thank you, Papa, and I promise that we will be together again soon." Rosebud gave her papa an extra big hug and kiss in return.

Once again, Mama and Rosebud crouched low and followed Dorothy out of the gazebo. Rosebud ran beside Mama, hiding in her shadow as planned. When they arrived at the basket, Dorothy grabbed Rosebud and lifted her into it. Mama stared in awe at the loaded basket. "There's no room for Rosebud," she whispered.

Dorothy searched for a hiding place for Rosebud and her belongings. "Look at this huge pile of clothing and food. You're right, Mama. There isn't any more room!" Dorothy exclaimed.

"There's no room for me, and there's no place to hide," Rosebud said, starting to cry.

"Don't worry, child," Mama said. "We'll think of something. We always do!"

"I have an idea," Rosebud said. "Let's make a tunnel in the pile of clothing, and I'll hide in it with my stuff. That way, if anyone comes near, they won't be able to see me."

"That's a wonderful idea," Dorothy whispered, making a tunnel large enough for Rosebud to crawl into.

Rosebud hid her clothing and food in the tunnel. She spoke with a hint of sadness in her voice. "I'm ready, Mama. I'm going to miss you, Papa, and my dear little Apricot, but I promise I'll be back a lot bigger person when I return."

"I know you will." Mama sighed and gave Rosebud one last hug and kiss.

"I'll see you tomorrow, Dorothy," Rosebud said with a wide grin.

Dorothy and Mama, crouching low, disappeared into the darkness. For a long time, Rosebud listened for an alarm to be sounded, but nothing happened. She knew they had made it safely out of Emerald City.

What will happen to me next? Will the Wizard of Oz discover me hiding in here before we take off? Will we make it to Kansas? If we get to Kansas, will I grow taller? Rosebud wondered about these things and more. Then she snuggled inside the tunnel and fell into a restless sleep.

CHAPTER V

APRICOT AND A GOOD WITCH

Rosebud was lying in the tunnel with her head outside the clothing, when something brushed against her cheek. She was wide awake instantly and covering her mouth to keep from screaming.

What was that? She thought, ducking quickly into the tunnel.

Whatever it was, this time it was peeking inside the tunnel and licking her face.

"Apricot, it's you!" Rosebud said, in a voice half-crying and half-laughing. She picked Apricot up and hid her in the tunnel. "You followed me here, didn't you, you naughty cat?"

Rosebud was very happy and comforted to have Apricot by her side.

"You'll have to be quiet, or we'll be in trouble," Rosebud warned.

Apricot seemed to understand what Rosebud was saying as the two of them crawled out of sight and huddled together deep inside the tunnel. Soon they were fast asleep. They hadn't been asleep very long when an eerie, glowing blue ball, about the size of a quarter, came into the tunnel and shone brightly in their eyes.

"Awake, my child, and follow me," the light beckoned as it left the tunnel.

Rosebud awakened with a start and, picking up Apricot, crawled out of the tunnel and stood on the floor of the basket. The glowing blue ball began to grow larger and larger until there before them stood the most beautiful lady Rosebud had ever seen. The beautiful lady was dressed in a long, flowing, sky blue gown accented with silver sequins. She wore dark blue satin slippers and carried a matching dark blue wand with a silver star at its tip. Her flowing blonde hair was laced with gorgeous blue butterflies and a white glowing halo was just above her head.

"Who are you, and what do you want?" Rosebud asked. Her eyes were as big as saucers. She rubbed them to see if the beautiful lady was real.

"I'm the Good Witch of the North, and I've been assigned to watch over and protect you on your journey." She bent over and placed a warm kiss on Rosebud's left cheek. "No one will dare harm you, or anyone with you, when they see this kiss I have placed on your cheek. You will not remember this when you wake up, but I'll be there if you need me."

The Good Witch of the North began to grow smaller and smaller until she was again the size of a quarter.

Then she vanished into the night. Rosebud reached out to touch the Good Witch and thank her, but it was too late. Rosebud and Apricot crawled back into their tunnel. *Was she real or a dream?* Rosebud fell into a deep sleep with Apricot purring contentedly in her arms.

CHAPTER VI

TOTO CAUSES HAVOC

The roar of the crowd, the crashing of cymbals, the banging of drums, and the blaring of horns rudely awakened Rosebud and Apricot. A startled Rosebud, forgetting she was sleeping in the tunnel, attempted to jump to her feet to see what the commotion was about. Her head hit the clothing, reminding her where she was.

Rosebud grabbed Apricot to prevent her from crying out or running out of the tunnel and giving them away. "Shh," she said, stroking Apricot's head to soothe her fears. "We have to be quiet."

Apricot understood and remained motionless and silent.

"Here they come!" someone shouted. A loud cheer went up from the crowd.

By turning her head slightly and separating the clothes, Rosebud was able to see through the small holes where the wickers of the basket were woven together.

"It's a parade," Rosebud whispered to Apricot. "The Wizard of Oz, Dorothy, Toto, Scarecrow, Tin Man, Cowardly Lion, and Mayor Mingle are leading the way, and they're heading straight toward us."

The parade stopped a few feet from the basket, and several of the marchers began to build a large, very hot fire. When the fire got big enough, they would catch the rising hot air from it and fill the balloon so it would fly into the sky.

The Wizard of Oz told the marchers, "Force as much hot air into the balloon as you possibly can. If we don't have enough hot air in the balloon and it cools too fast, we'll land in the desert."

While the balloon was being filled with hot air, Mayor Mingle decided to orate about the wonderful Wizard of Oz and how much everyone looked forward to his return. Meanwhile, Rosebud could feel the heat from the fire and see the hot air rising into the balloon. Her heart was beating like a drum. *Hurry,* she thought, *before I pass out from the heat.*

After Mayor Mingle finished speaking, he turned the podium over to the Wizard of Oz, who thanked everyone for coming and promised them that he would return after delivering Dorothy to Kansas. Unbeknownst to the crowd, the Wizard of Oz had no intention of ever coming back to Emerald City and having them discover he was not really a true wizard. After he finished speaking, he waved and stepped into the basket. The crowd clapped and shouted, and a voice called out, "We're going to miss you, Wizard of Oz. Please hurry back."

While the Wizard was talking, Dorothy walked over to the basket to check on Rosebud.

"Are you okay, Rosebud?" Dorothy asked.

"I'm very warm, but I'm doing all right. Let's get going," Rosebud urged.

The balloon was now half full, and the wind was causing the basket, which by now had risen about a foot off of the ground, to tip precariously from side to side. Rosebud and Apricot became panicky thinking that the basket might fall over and spill them out. Their fears were eased when several Munchkins grabbed the mooring ropes and held the basket in place.

"It won't be long now, Apricot," Rosebud whispered. "Soon we'll be on our way to Kansas."

It was now Dorothy's turn to make a speech. Dorothy thanked the townspeople for their kindness and promised she would never forget them. She finished her speech, picked up Toto, and sat on the edge of the basket beside the Wizard of Oz. Their added weight helped to stabilize the balloon, which was almost full of hot air and tugging hard against the mooring ropes. Liftoff would take place any moment.

Toto spotted a cat in the crowd, jumped from Dorothy's arms, and ran after it.

Dorothy stepped off of the basket and began chasing Toto. She finally caught him and turned to get back into the basket.

The balloon was now so filled with hot air that those holding the mooring ropes could no longer hang on, and without Dorothy's added weight, up it went. The

Wizard of Oz attempted to grab Dorothy's hand and pull her into the basket, but he missed.

"Come back. Come back. Wait for me," Dorothy shouted.

"I can't come back. I don't know how. Good luck getting to Kansas," the Wizard of Oz shouted back. He waved to Dorothy and Toto as the balloon rose higher.

"Good luck to you, Wizard of Oz. Have a safe journey," Dorothy yelled, and waved goodbye.

No sooner had Dorothy said this, when, unexpectedly, the balloon caught a downdraft and headed back to earth toward the startled crowd. Everyone was reaching for the mooring ropes to pull the basket down so that Dorothy and Toto could get in. They jumped high in the air but couldn't quite reach the ropes. Just then, a passing wind caught the balloon and sent it scurrying down the yellow brick road.

"Hurry!" ordered the Wizard of Oz. "Grab the ropes and hold the basket down. If I reach the cliffs at the end of the yellow brick road, I may crash into the valley far below." But it was too late.

The chase was on.

The giant balloon was moving slowly, about a foot above the yellow brick road.

"Stop right where you are." Mayor Mingle thought his command would make the balloon stop. After all, he was the mayor.

Everyone was trying to catch the mooring ropes that were dragging along the ground. But the ropes seemed to be playing a game of tag with the pursuers by staying just out of their reach.

"The balloon is about to climb up the high hill to the cliffs," Mayor Mingle yelled."If we're going to stop it and get Dorothy and Toto on board, we have to do it now."

Scarecrow grabbed the hat off of his head and tucked it under his arm. He began sprinting like an Olympic runner going for the gold. He grabbed a mooring rope as the balloon started up the high hill. "I've got it. I've got it," Scarecrow screamed. However, being filled with straw, he wasn't heavy enough to slow down, or stop the balloon. "I'm going to wrap my long legs around that large boulder ahead and stop this ornery balloon. Then the rest of you can grab on."

Scarecrow grabbed onto the boulder with his legs and screeched, "Hey, I can't stop this balloon. My arms have been torn off, and my hat has blown away." This didn't hurt him, but it would take the rest of the day to sew his arms on and fill them with straw.

Next to reach the balloon was Tin Man. "I've got it," he yelled, making a frantic dive.

He managed to grab a single rope and hang on. His weight began to slow the balloon down. "I'm not heavy enough to stop this thing. I need help now." He was waving and flailing his ax.

Tin Man was dragged along the ground and into the path of a boulder. He hit the boulder with such force that he was tossed into the air like a pancake and flipped upside down. Tin Man landed on his back, and his flailing ax cut the mooring rope he was holding in half. He sat on the ground, holding the other half of the rope and watched the balloon move closer to the top of the hill and its unknown fate.

Only one hope was left to stop the balloon, and that was the Cowardly Lion. Cowardly Lion had the grace, speed, courage, and strength to bring the balloon down and hold it until they could board Dorothy and Toto. "It won't escape my clutches," he roared, racing like the wind up the high hill. He reached the balloon and leaped high into the air. He was about to grab the mooring rope in his massive jaws when Tin Man stood up, waving the other half of the mooring rope he had cut off. Cowardly Lion got his feet tangled in the piece of rope and fell to the ground, rolling over and over. They could only watch the balloon fly out above the cliffs and rise high into the air.

Everyone waved goodbye and wished the Wizard of Oz a safe journey.

A passing wind caught the balloon and pushed it toward an unknown journey. The Wizard of Oz and his stowaways were on their way to the vast, hot desert. Next stop,

Kansas?

I wonder if the Wizard of Oz will throw me and Apricot out of the balloon when he finds us? Rosebud thought, pushing deeper into the tunnel.

CHAPTER VII

TWO TINY STOWAWAYS

The balloon sailed high and fast and was soon flying over the barren, hot desert. The excitement of the morning had made the Wizard of Oz very hungry. He reached into his food basket for one of his famous sandwiches made of peanut butter, grape jelly, cooked cabbage, mayonnaise, and sardines. The Wizard of Oz had named this sandwich the bagurgle because of the strange noises it made whenever you took a bite out of it. This was his favorite food, and he had packed several bagurgle sandwiches for the journey.

Forlorn and lonely, the Wizard of Oz stood looking out over the desert. He was eating his bagurgle sandwich, and the juices from the grape jelly, mayonnaise, and sardines were running down his hands and onto his arms. This was the problem with the bagurgle. It was very messy, and you had to sit down to eat it, or you would wind up wearing it. The only place the Wizard of Oz could sit was on the pile of clothing where Rosebud and Apricot were hiding. He sat down with a weary, "Kerplop!"

"Ouch!" cried a muffled voice.

The startled Wizard of Oz leaped to his feet shrieking, "Who said that? Who's there?"

There was no answer.

Thinking the voice he had heard was his imagination, or the wind howling, the Wizard of Oz again sat down on the pile of clothing.

"Get off me, you big ox," the pile of clothing shouted.

The Wizard of Oz leaped to his feet. He jumped up so fast that he lost his grip and dropped the rest of his bagurgle sandwich over the side of the basket. He grabbed at the sandwich but missed. All he could do was watch his precious bagurgle sandwich spatter on the desert floor far below. The Wizard of Oz knew for certain that he was not alone in the basket. His heart was hammering like a bass drum leading a parade, and his mouth was drier than a bale of cotton. He wet his lips and shouted, "Come out of there right now and there won't be any trouble."

Rosebud, fearing for their lives, pressed Apricot closer to her and pushed as far as she could into the tunnel. The Wizard of Oz stared at his shiny, knee-high black boots that were sitting on top of the pile of clothing. He clutched the toe of the boots and, lifting them off of the pile, turned them upside down and gave them a hearty slap on the soles. No one popped out, or made any noise.

Next, the Wizard of Oz lifted his red wool pants with the red suspenders, cautiously squeezed the pant legs, and ran his hand to the bottom of every pocket. No one!

Then he gingerly picked up the red wool coat that he wore in the coldest of weather. He ran his arms through the sleeves, along the lining, and checked every pocket. No one!

"Hmm!" the Wizard of Oz said, giving his red wool mittens, hat, and muffler a hearty shake. No one!

He turned pale, a chill went up his spine, and goose bumps popped up all over his body. Only one garment was left that was large enough for someone, or something, to crawl into and hide. It was his warm, woolly, red long johns with the trap door. The Wizard of Oz backed away from the long johns, not knowing what or whom to expect. He had no place hide! The balloon was more than one thousand feet above the desert, so he couldn't jump from the basket without being killed. *If I were a true wizard, I could turn myself into a bird and fly away,* he thought.

Trying to be as brave as possible, the Wizard of Oz shouted in a jittery voice, "I know you're in there. You better come out right now."

Apricot, not wanting Rosebud to get hurt, pushed out of her arms, and crawled up through the trap door of the long johns. She faced the Wizard of Oz, hissing, back arched, left paw flailing like a lion resisting a lion tamer.

The Wizard of Oz breathed a sigh of relief knowing that a tiny cat had caused the problem. "Well, what have we here?" he asked, picking up the hissing Apricot. He massaged Apricot's head to settle her down and realized that, *Cats don't talk. Someone else has to be on board. But who could it be?* Once again panic set in.

Rosebud, fearing something terrible was about to happen to Apricot, climbed out of their hiding place. "Please, don't hurt Apricot, or me," she pleaded, grabbing her cat away from the Wizard of Oz.

"Why, my dear child, I wouldn't think of hurting the poor little creature. Nor would I think of harming you either."

"You mean you won't throw us out of the basket?"

"Of course I won't. In fact, I welcome the company. Where are you going?"

"Oh, great Wizard of Oz, don't you remember me? I'm Rosebud. I came to you yesterday and asked if I could fly to Kansas with you and Dorothy so I could grow taller. You refused to let me fly with you, because the basket was already overloaded. So, during the night, Dorothy stowed me away in the clothing. Look at me. I'm a mini Munchkin."

Rosebud laughed at her little joke. "I just want to go to Kansas, eat corn, and grow to be the same size, or taller than the other Munchkins."

"Oh yes, now I remember. Without Dorothy and Toto, we have plenty of room in the basket, so you can stay. My problem is that I don't know where Kansas is or what it looks like. Do you know? And by the way, Rosebud, please don't call me the Wizard of Oz. From now on, you can call me Wizard."

"Okay, Wizard! Dorothy told me that Kansas is grayer than a dark sky filled with rain clouds. She said that even the people and farms are gray. If we keep a sharp eye from up here, we should be able to spot it."

"Let's hope we see Kansas before it gets dark tonight, or in tomorrow's first daylight. Then we can land and find Dorothy's farm."

"Wizard, what will happen to us when we land? Will we crash?"

"If the hot air cools gradually, we'll come down safely and have a soft landing. Otherwise, we may fall like a stone and be injured, or perhaps something worse."

"I'm scared," said Rosebud, staring intently in every direction, hoping to see Kansas or the end of the desert.

CHAPTER VIII

DANCING ON THE TREE TOPS

"Well, Rosebud," said the Wizard of Oz. "We've been flying without incident for several hours, and neither of us has spotted Kansas or the end of the desert. This could be a problem, because the sun is setting rapidly and soon night will be upon us. We may fly over Kansas and not know it!"

"Where did that huge, brilliant rainbow come from?" the Wizard asked, pointing north. "It's so bright maybe we can drop down and find the pot of gold," he joked.

"I wonder if Kansas is somewhere over the rainbow." "There's a land that I dream of," a teary eyed Rosebud sighed.

At that moment, a bolt of lightning came out of nowhere, struck the rainbow, and blew it into a million colorful prisms. The prisms flew like feathers in the wind and popped like bubbles in a bathtub when they struck the desert floor. The basket was rocked back and forth.

Thunder followed the bolt of lightning and sounded like a long, loud, evil laugh. "Go back. Go back to where you came from, or you'll be next," the rumbling, thunderous voice bellowed.

"Did you hear that voice?" Rosebud asked. Apricot pushed hard against her leg.

"Yes indeed," the Wizard said. He had a stunned expression on his face. "What, or whom, do you think it is, Wizard?"

"I don't have any idea. The desert is full of mirages. Maybe that was one? It's getting dark, Rosebud. It's time you and Apricot got some rest. Sleep on the pile of clothing, and I'll keep watching for Kansas."

Rosebud and Apricot curled up under a blanket of stars that twinkled like billions of diamonds in the night. They were hypnotized by the stars rushing by, and soon fell fast asleep.

The Wizard stared in wonder at the desert floor. It had taken on an eerie gray aura created by the light of the stars. He thought, *Perhaps the desert floor is now the same color gray as the state of Kansas. I'll keep a closer watch and search for lighted farmhouses and barns.*

His constant staring at the desert floor had caused the Wizard's eyes to grow heavy. He had to work hard to keep alert. The Wizard began to sing, dance, and talk out loud to stay awake.

It wasn't long before the constant drone of the air rushing by, and the rising heat of the day affected the Wizard. He abruptly stopped singing, dancing, and talking out loud. The darkness of the earth below, and the glitter of the stars above, had put the Wizard into a sleepy trance. Though standing quite erect, with his right hand over his eyes for a better view, the Wizard had fallen fast asleep.

The first rays of the morning sun rising over the desert struck the Wizard in the face, causing him to panic. He awoke with a start to the sounds of something scraping the bottom of the basket.

What on earth is that strange scraping noise, and why is the basket rocking? The Wizard wondered, peering down to see what was below them.

To his horror, the Wizard discovered that while he was sleeping, the balloon had crossed the desert, lost most of its hot air, and was descending into a dense black forest. The scraping noise was made by the basket dancing along the treetops.

He screamed, "Rosebud, Apricot, wake up and hang on. We're crashing into the treetops of a forest."

Rosebud, hearing the Wizard's screams, grabbed onto the side of the basket and hung on tight. Apricot dug her claws into the pile of clothing and hid her head in one of the Wizard's big black boots.

"Hold on tight to the basket and don't let go. We could get caught in the treetops and be spilled out onto the forest floor." the Wizard warned.

"What's going to happen to us?" Rosebud cried.

Before the Wizard could answer, the basket cleared the treetops and came to light with a soft bump in an open, grassy, forest glade. Most of the hot air had gone out of the balloon, and it flopped down beside them.

Then, with what seemed like one last gasp, the balloon gave a long hiss and went completely flat.

"Whew, that was close!" The Wizard laughed nervously. "A few minutes sooner and we'd have been hung up in the trees."

"Where are we?" Rosebud asked.

"I don't have any idea, Rosebud," said the Wizard." "All I can tell you is that we're lost in a grassy glade in an unknown dense black forest."

Chapter IX

In the Land of the Tawnies

"Luckily, we made it across the desert before we came down," Rosebud said, climbing out of the basket. "Did you see Kansas, or in which direction we need to travel to find it?"

"No, Rosebud. Unfortunately, I didn't see anything. I'm embarrassed to say that I fell fast asleep. I woke up when the bright morning sun hit me in the eyes, and then I heard the sound of the basket scraping the trees."

"That's all right. It's not your fault you fell asleep. We were very tired from our busy day. I should have helped you to stay awake. We'll be all right. You'll see." Rosebud comforted the Wizard, patting him gently on the back.

"We better load up what we can carry and start walking," the Wizard said, picking up some clothing, food, and water.

Rosebud gathered supplies for herself and Apricot. Then she placed Apricot into the backpack. "I'm ready. Which way are we going?"

"Pick one," replied the Wizard, searching for an opening through the forest. "Make sure you choose the right one, or we may wander in circles in this black forest, and that could be the end for us."

"You know, Wizard, if we had a compass, we could make sure we're not traveling in circles."

"AHA, you've got it, Rosebud! You see, moss always grows on the north side of a tree. Let's follow the moss to the north, and perhaps it will lead us out of this forest."

"Good idea, Wizard. Here's some moss."

They hadn't followed the moss very far when they came upon a dirt road.

"It worked, Rosebud. The moss led us out of the forest. It's a miracle." The Wizard danced with glee, kicking up circles of dust as he hopped up and down on the dirt road.

"Do we get to Kansas by going up this dirt road, or down this dirt road?" a puzzled Rosebud asked.

"It doesn't matter which way we go, Rosebud, because we don't know where we are. However, I can see down the dirt road a long way, and there's no one to help us. I can't see up the dirt road because of the hill. So let's go up the dirt road and over the hill. Perhaps we'll run into someone who can tell us which direction to go."

They walked to the top of the hill.

"Stop," warned the Wizard, grabbing Rosebud's arm. "Do you see those strange looking people working in that field of yellow cotton?"

Rosebud peeked out from behind the Wizard's leg. "I see them," she whispered. "What do we do now?"

"Follow me," said the Wizard. The two of them scurried down the hill and hid behind a tree. They stared at the strange looking people wondering who they were.

"Do you see how funny they're dressed?" Rosebud asked.

"Yes indeed I do. They're wearing tall, yellow, cone-shaped hats, and high-heeled black boots that reach their knees."

"Do you think they're friendly?"

"I don't know. You stay behind this tree and I'll find out. Whatever you do, Rosebud, don't show yourself, unless I call or wave for you to come out." The Wizard bravely stepped out from behind the tree and walked onto the dirt road. He was shaking like a bowl of jelly.

The Wizard hailed them. "Hello, you people working in the field. I'm lost. Are you friendly, and can you give me directions?"

"You're in the land of Saffron. We are the very friendly people known as the Tawnies. Are you friendly, too?" asked a man with a long yellow beard.

"Yes, I am!"

"My name is Bisque Tawnie. I'm the leader here. And we'll be overjoyed to help you in any way we can. Please tell me who you are, and where you want to go. Perhaps I can point you in the right direction." By this time, Bisque had walked out of the field and was standing next to the Wizard.

"I'm the Wizard of Oz," he said, waving Rosebud out from behind the tree.

"You're the great Wizard of Oz? We've heard of the miracles you worked with our friends, Tin Man, Scarecrow, and the Cowardly Lion. Welcome to our humble land." Bisque bowed to the Wizard.

Rosebud stepped out warily from behind the tree, holding Apricot in her arms. She stood behind the Wizard, peeking around his left leg at Bisque.

"It's okay, Rosebud. They're a friendly people known as the Tawnies," the Wizard assured her.

Rosebud moved out from behind the Wizard's leg and gave Bisque a friendly smile and a curtsy. Bisque stared at Rosebud and Apricot. He had never seen a person or cat so small.

"Who's the little lady and cat with you?" Bisque asked, bowing back to Rosebud.

"This is Rosebud and her cat Apricot. They're traveling with me to Kansas. Do you know where Kansas is, Bisque?"

"Kansas? I've never heard of it. What is it? Can it be eaten?"

"Kansas is a large, gray-colored place, and that's the only thing we know about it."

"I can't help you. I've never been to Kansas. How did the three of you get here? Are there more of you?"

"There aren't any more of us. We got here in my hot air balloon. During the cool night, the balloon ran out of hot air and landed somewhere in a grassy, open space in a dense black forest. But I don't have any idea where that is."

"It sounds to me like you landed at Lemony Forest Glade. Why don't you put some more hot air in your balloon and go on your way to Kansas?"

"I need at least a dozen men to assist in building a large fire so we can fill the balloon with hot air. Do you think that you and the other Tawnies in the field can help me?"

"Certainly," Bisque replied. "Let's do it!"

Bisque took a small yellow horn out of his pocket and blew on it. The horn made a delightful sound like the singing of canaries. The Tawnies immediately put down their hoes, rakes, and shovels and came running to Bisque. They stood at attention awaiting his instructions.

Bisque told his men who their visitors were and of the Wizard's problem. "Tawnies, follow me to the balloon," Bisque ordered, marching up the dirt road. And they did.

"We don't have to build a fire," Bisque told the Wizard. "We can build you fuel tanks and fill them with gas. We've done it many times for our tractors. We're not only farmers, we're tinsmiths, too."

"Are you sure you can build fuel tanks that will work on my balloon?" the Wizard asked.

"Of course we can! Why, we put the busted up Tin Man back together like new only a few days ago," Bisque bragged.

"Then do it!" The Wizard danced with delight at the thought of new fuel tanks.

By this time, they had arrived at the forest glade. Bisque instructed the workers. "Pick up the basket and the balloon and carry them to the village."

The Tawnies placed the balloon and basket behind the blacksmith shop where they kept their tools and supplies. Then they immediately began measuring the basket and making new fuel tanks.

"It will take us several hours to build the fuel tanks, but we should finish by morning," said Bisque. "In the meantime, you can stay at Mrs. Taddle Tawnie's bed and breakfast. It's across the street. We'll come and get you when we're done."

The Wizard thanked the Tawnies for their help. Then he, Rosebud, and Apricot walked across the street to find rooms for the night. They had no idea of the wonderful surprise the Tawnies were preparing for them.

The next morning, the Tawnies blindfolded the Wizard and brought him to see the big surprise.

"Wow!" exclaimed the Wizard when the blindfold was removed. "I can't believe it! This is the most magnificent silver basket and silver balloon I've ever seen, and they're again as large as my old ones."

"We Tawnies have made the basket and balloon of fine, lightweight, silver-meshed metal threads," Bisque said. "Silver fuel tanks have been installed in the four corners with silver metal heat pipes leading to the balloon. We built a silver table for two in one corner and a tiny silver cathouse for Apricot in another. We also built a silver storage chest and put your clothing and supplies in it."

"I can't believe how light this is," Rosebud said, picking up one corner of the basket.

"The tanks are filled with fuel and ready to fire," Bisque said. He and the other Tawnies wore big satisfied smiles on their faces.

"Bisque, before we go, I need to ask you a question," said the Wizard.

"What is it, Wizard, and why the worried expression on your face?"

"Have you ever heard of a rainbow appearing in the sky and being blasted to bits by lightning?"

"I sure have," said Bisque. "It is said that an evil wizard by the name of Shanevil lurks in the Alp mountains. He is known to use lightning to destroy anyone or anything that approaches his home. Don't go near it, whatever you do. However, he cannot fly, so if the wind is right, you can easily escape in your balloon. Also, a good Wizard named, Shagoodie, dwells in the Alps. If you get into trouble with Shanevil, call out his name and he will come to your aid."

There were hugs, kisses and handshakes all around. Rosebud climbed up the tiny silver ladder and placed Apricot in her silver cathouse. The Wizard stepped into the basket, opened the gas valves, and lit the pipes. The balloon was now filled with hot air and trying to rise up from the ground.

"Thank you, Tawnies, for your help!" The Wizard shook hands all around. "It will be our pleasure to pay you back some day."

"Do a good deed for others in need, and you'll have paid us back indeed," Bisque yelled above the roar of the fired up fuel tanks.

"We'll do kind deeds for others in honor of you Tawnies," Rosebud shouted.

"Release the mooring ropes," the Wizard commanded.

The Tawnies immediately released the mooring ropes. They all waved as the balloon rose into the air. The Wizard and Rosebud continued to wave right back at the Tawnies until they were out of sight.

"Wow, Rosebud! Isn't this marvelous? With these new tanks we won't have to land until we get to Kansas."

The Wizard, Rosebud, and Apricot flew steadily on a north wind for another seven days. Although they kept a constant watch, day and night, they didn't spot Kansas, or anything that resembled it. The terrain below was alive with green grass, trees, and blue waters, but no Kansas gray.

Every night at seven o'clock, a gigantic rainbow would appear ahead of them. The rainbow would be struck by a terrorizing bolt of lightning and blasted into millions of rainbow-colored prisms.

The thunder that followed sounded like a long, loud, evil laugh. The thunderous message was always the same, "Go back to where you came from, or you'll be blasted from the sky."

"Rosebud, there's no way I can make the balloon change direction. Only the wind can do that, and it's not cooperating. It's like a giant magnet is pulling us north and I'm helpless to do anything about it. I'm afraid that if this wind doesn't change direction soon, we'll be flying into a death trap."

"Wizard how soon do you think it will be before we're blasted out of the sky and turned into human prisms?" a trembling Rosebud asked.

CHAPTER X

INTO THE FOG BANK OF DEATH

On the tenth day, Rosebud pointed and said, "Wizard, I see some very tall, snow covered mountains ahead. Do you suppose they're the Alps?"

"I hope not, because if they are, we're heading directly to the evil Shanevil's home."

That evening, the rainbow, the lightning, and the thunderous booming voice were stronger than ever.

On the eleventh day, everything but the snow covered tops of the mountains disappeared under a giant fog bank.

"Wizard, where did that fog bank come from?" Rosebud asked. "It wasn't there a few minutes ago. Do you think it was caused by Shanevil?"

"Possibly, but I don't think so. A fog bank rolls in and out of these mountains quite often especially in the mornings. I don't believe the fog was caused by

Shanevil, since he wants to keep an eye on us. I consider the fog bank to be our friend because, if we have to, we can hide in it until it's safe to escape."

"Let's fly over the mountains and escape before it's too late and the fog bank goes away," Rosebud said.

"We can't go over the tops of the mountains. We have to wait for the fog bank to disappear. What if Kansas is at the base of one of the mountains and we miss it?"

At that moment, a rainbow so dazzling that it almost blinded them arched directly over the balloon. No sooner had it appeared when, "Kaboom," it was struck by a bolt of lightning and blown into millions of rainbow-colored prisms. The lightning bolt was so close they could feel the heat, and it made their hair stand on end.

Some of the prisms popped when they floated down and struck the top of the balloon. Others gradually floated down and popped when they landed on the Wizard and Rosebud. Apricot playfully flailed her paws at the prisms that reached the basket floor.

They waited intently for the booming voice, only to be greeted by an eerie silence.

"What on earth is happening? Where is the warning voice? Are we next?" the frightened Wizard whispered.

Rosebud was holding her nose. "What's that awful smell, and where is it coming from?"

An icy cold wind blew across their faces and down their shaking bodies. They clung to each other in fear and tried to keep warm.

"Do you suppose that this is the end?" Rosebud asked.

"I'm afraid that something terrible is about to happen to us," muttered the Wizard.

Then, a voice so shrill it made their blood run cold came from out of the fog bank, "You've been warned. You're not welcome here. I've given you every chance to go away, or else, and you have refused to go. Why?"

"Believe me," the Wizard replied, "if I had the power to control the wind, I would have gladly turned this balloon around and gone back to where we came from."

"Oh great one," Rosebud spoke in a trembling voice, "you possess awesome powers. You're able to create thunder and lightning. I have no doubt that one as powerful as you can change the direction of the wind. If you'll do that then we can be gone and fly to Kansas."

"Your request has come too late. You're doomed." A bolt of lightning flew out of the fog bank, narrowly missing the basket. It was followed by a shrill laugh.

Rosebud and the Wizard stared with dread at the spot in the dense fog from which the voice and lightning had shot out. Creeping terror gripped them, and they wondered how soon they would die?

The icy raw chill drifting across their bodies intensified. They felt like they were in a deep freeze. Their fingers, toes, and noses became numb. They tried to speak but their mouths were too dry. Their eyes bulged in horror when they saw the monster that was floating out of the fog bank. It was heading directly toward them. They were so paralyzed with fear that they couldn't bend down to hide behind the walls of the basket.

A pencil-shaped nose began to appear, dripping like a bad faucet. It was tall as the tallest tree with a wart the size of a garbage pail on the end of it. Ugly sunken cheeks, the color of dark green watermelons followed the nose. One cheek was oozing dark red blood and yellow and purple puss from an open sore, perhaps caused by an earlier encounter. Then, from out of the dense fog appeared eyebrows, beard, and hair, looking and smelling like rotting weeds in a stagnant pond. The monster's mustache and beard were matted with the constant drippings from its nose. The nose drippings were spread by bony, wart-covered hands with six-inch long fingernails. The hands massaged the drippings into the hair on top of the monster's head. Doing this made the hair smell like it had been slicked down with lard from a festering pig.

Next, a ghastly mouth appeared with brown drool hanging from its corners. Large cankered and cracked puffy lips surrounded the mouth and gave forth a haunting grin. The monster's gums were full of black decaying teeth and a black split tongue. A stench rose from its breath that was so bad only maggots could live in such a horrible mouth—and they did.

The monster had no ear lobes. They had been chewed away by the snakes and rats that perched on its shoulders. Though it seemed that the monster had penetrating eyes, there were none. Where eyes should have been were empty sockets that glowed like low-burning candles. This was the ugliest, most foul-smelling thing the Wizard of Oz or Rosebud had ever seen.

Emerging totally from the fog, the hideous image grew to enormous heights and glared at the balloon and its occupants like they were a box of candy, waiting to be devoured. Rosebud and the Wizard stared numb with fear. The creature began floating directly toward them, shrinking rapidly as it got closer and closer. It shrank to ten feet in height and stopped a few feet from the basket, fire coming from its dark and penetrating empty eye sockets.

Rosebud and the Wizard fell to the floor and covered their faces in an attempt to get away from the foul-smelling breath. They began coughing and gagging from the stench. Apricot leaped into her cage and hid her head in the corner, her tail, and the fur on her back, standing straight up.

The creature wore a cape and had a large black rat sitting on top of his head. Its robe was made of live snakes and rats that hissed and squealed at Rosebud and the Wizard. The cone-shaped hat was adorned with black, evil-looking bats. Apricot cowered deep in the corner of her cage, afraid to move. She feared that the rats and snakes would see her, jump into the basket, and devour her.

"Who are you?" the Wizard of Oz asked in his most courageous voice. The Wizard's knees were shaking so hard, they sounded like a bag of marbles being dropped on a wooden floor. He had all he could do to keep from falling over in a dead faint.

"I'm the Wizard Shanevil," the monster answered, his blazing eye sockets shooting flames at them.

"H...H...Hello, Mr. Shanevil. My name's Rosebud and I'm happy to meet you." She too was ready to faint.

"I'm the Wizard of Oz, and I'm happy to meet you, too," he said with a bow.

"There can only be *one* Wizard in these mountains, and that one is *me*!" Shanevil's booming voice was so loud that it bounced the basket up and down like a rubber ball.

"We...we mean you no harm, Shanevil," the Wizard of Oz said. "And I gratefully accept that you are the only wizard allowed in these mountains. We are passing this way trying to find a place called Kansas. Have you ever heard of Kansas? Do you know where it is?" Shanevil's fiery eye sockets blazed at him like he was a marshmallow on a stick about to be roasted over an open campfire.

Shanevil floated a short distance away from the balloon and gave an evil laugh. The fire intensified in his empty eye sockets. Then he pointed at the sky and directed a bolt of lightning out of his fingernails and over the top of the balloon. The Wizard of Oz and Rosebud hugged each other in terror.

"I don't know of a place called Kansas. Be aware that if you enter these mountains with your airship, you will never leave them alive. I promise."

"Oh great Wizard Shanevil, please change the direction the wind is blowing," the Wizard of Oz pleaded.

Shanevil ignored the Wizard of Oz's request and said, "I have fired off all but one of my lightning bolts, and it has made me very weary. I must go to my ice castle now and recharge my batteries. If you dare to enter my mountains while I'm sleeping, then, when I awake, "Kapow!" he said, drawing his bony fingers across his neck like a knife.

Before Shanevil left, he directed his last bolt of lightning under the basket. The heat from the lightning caused the metal floor to get so hot that the three of them had to dance like puppets on a string to keep their feet from burning.

"Don't be here when I wake up, or you're fried." Shanevil laughed, watching them dance. He once again grew into a giant monster and melted back into the fog bank.

The Wizard of Oz and Rosebud stared for a long time at the fog bank where Shanevil had disappeared.

"I thought the evil Shanevil couldn't fly?" said Rosebud.

"I don't believe he can. He can only float on the air. Otherwise, he would have flown out and fried us a few days ago. I wonder how long it takes for him to recharge his batteries?"

"Wizard, how much time do we have before we enter the fog bank, and what can we do to save ourselves?"

"We'll be in the fog bank in about twenty minutes, and there's nothing we can do to save ourselves. It's over!" a terrified Wizard of Oz replied.

"We're doomed," wailed Rosebud.

CHAPTER XI

WE'VE BEEN STRUCK

"Be prepared, Rosebud, we're about to enter the fog bank," the Wizard said. The balloon drifted into the fog bank and instantly disappeared from sight. An eerie green glow totally engulfed them as they traveled deeper and deeper into the mystifying fog.

"Wizard," a frantic Rosebud said, "this is like being in a cave. I can't see up, down, or sideways, and I can barely see you. What's going to happen to us? Are we going to die?"

The Wizard, trying to calm Rosebud, held her close to comfort her, and said, "Rosebud, I don't know in which direction we're traveling. I also don't know what's below or above us, or worse yet, if we'll crash into the side of a mountain and be killed. So here's what you need to do to protect yourself. Hang on tight to the side of the basket and whatever you do, don't let go."

"I won't, Wizard, but I wonder if the evil Shanevil knows that we've floated into the fog bank?"

"Something's wrong," the Wizard warned. "I don't feel the wind anymore. We're at a dead standstill."

"Do you suppose evil Shanevil has caused the wind to stop blowing?" Rosebud whispered. She was afraid that Shanevil might hear her and blast them into tiny floating prisms.

"Could be," the Wizard whispered back. " Maybe he's recharged his batteries, and is preparing to hit us with a deadly bolt of lightning."

They both listened intently, trying to discover where Shanevil was lurking.

The Wizard whispered, "We're caught in the Alps in a dead wind with fog so thick I wouldn't be surprised if we could walk on it."

"You go first," said a smiling Rosebud. "What do we do now?"

"I don't dare try to land because I don't know what's below us. Besides, when we landed, I wouldn't have any idea which direction we should take to get to Kansas."

Then a strange noise pierced the fog.

"Shhh, listen," Rosebud said. "I hear someone snoring? Do you think that it's evil Shanevil?"

The Wizard listened to the snoring. "I hope it's him."

"If it's him, how can we get out of this fog before he wakes up and destroys us?" Rosebud whispered.

"I don't know, but we better think of something fast."

I know what we can do. How about if we . . ." Before the Wizard could finish what he was saying, a large unknown object struck the balloon and punched a hole in it. Air was escaping, and the balloon was slowly dropping down to whatever waited for them below.

"We've been struck by lightning and we're going to die!" Rosebud shrieked.

"I don't think so," the Wizard said. He was attempting, without success, to fill the balloon with air. "If Shanevil struck us with lightning, the balloon would have been blown to bits and us with it. It has to be something else. Quick, Rosebud, climb up the ropes and see if you can find the hole in the balloon, and what caused it. Let me know if it can be repaired. If the hole's not too big, we can plug it and escape from whatever is waiting beneath us."

"I'm on my way," said Rosebud, grabbing onto a rope.

Before Rosebud could climb up the rope, a flying reindeer fell into the basket, almost landing on top of her.

"Ouch!" the reindeer cried. "I bumped into something and hurt my leg. Can you help me to my feet," she asked.

"What on earth are you doing flying around in this fog?" the Wizard asked, helping the injured reindeer to her feet.

"I'm Dee, the flying reindeer," she told them, holding up her injured left front leg.

"Didn't you realize you could get hurt in this fog?" Rosebud said.

"I'm trying to earn my wings so I can fly over the Alp Mountains and rescue animals and people stranded in the snow. This is my tenth lesson, and I still can't figure out in which direction I'm going. I got lost in this big fog bank, and the next thing I knew, Bang! I ran into your cloud and fell into your basket. Lucky for me, your cloud is soft, or I might have been killed!"

"This isn't a cloud," Rosebud said. "It's a flying balloon. Probably the reason you didn't see our balloon is because it's silver, the same color as the fog."

"Yes, that's it exactly! But my instructors will blame me for getting lost in this fog. We students are forbidden from flying around in it." Dee was groaning from the pain in her injured left leg.

"If you're not supposed to fly in the fog, then why did you do it?" Rosebud asked.

"I wanted to see what it was like to fly in a fog bank, so I took a chance and went in.

It was my intention to fly right back out again. Before I could fly out, I hit your balloon with my hoof, and here I am."

"You should pay attention to what you are told. Then you wouldn't have so many problems," the Wizard said.

"That's my biggest fault. I don't pay enough attention to what I'm doing. Every time I go on a training mission, I get lost, or something bad happens to me, then the other trainees in my fleet have to stop their lessons and try to find me."

"If we could, we would scream and blow whistles so the other trainees could find you," the Wizard said. "However, if we make too much noise, we might wake up the evil wizard Shanevil, and he'll blast us out of the sky with a bolt of lightning."

Rosebud gave Dee's head a loving pat. "Is there anything else we can do to help you?" she asked.

"I'll be in a real pickle unless I can get back to my base before my instructors miss me. I need to use every one of my legs in order to take off and land safely. Perhaps you can fix my hurt leg for me, or maybe use your balloon to fly me home?"

"We can't fly you home, but maybe I can fix your leg so you can fly yourself home," said the Wizard. He tenderly lifted Dee's leg and began feeling for the injury.

"Yeow! That's the spot." Dee winced in pain.

"Dee," the Wizard told her, "you have a very bad sprain. I'm going to wrap your leg with duct tape, and maybe it will be strong enough for you to fly out of here."

"Oh thank you, Wizard. You are so kind to me."

The Wizard wrapped Dee's leg, "How does that feel?" he asked.

"It's still too painful for me to take off or land."

"Well, Dee, we'll have to worry about your sprained leg later. Right now we have a bigger problem. If we don't fix the hole that you poked in the balloon, we're liable to smack down on the earth so hard it will break all of our legs. Hurry, Rosebud, climb up and see how badly the balloon is damaged. We're beginning to drop faster, and we need to plug that hole, now."

"I'm on my way, Wizard." Rosebud scampered up the ropes to check the damage. "I found the hole, and it's too big to plug. I'm going to pull the torn ends together and slow down our descent. That way, maybe we'll survive when we crash."

Rosebud grabbed the two ripped ends and pulled them together. The balloon slowed its fall, but not enough.

"Dee, do you have any idea where we are, or what we might crash into below?" the Wizard asked.

"We're either flying over a mountain peak or a valley. I can't tell exactly which, because I can't see through this fog."

The fog began to thin as they dropped down the side of an ice-covered cliff. The ice was pure and as clear as glass. They could see right through it into a cave. Inside the cave, much to their relief was the evil Shanevil, still sound asleep.

"Someone else is inside the ice castle in a room next to Shanevil's. Whoever it is, they're waving to us." Dee pointed.

"Maybe it's the good wizard Shagoodie. The one Bisque spoke of?" Rosebud said.

"It appears to me that the person is in an ice prison," said Dee.

The person in the ice prison appeared to be a kindly wizard. He wore a cone-shaped hat and long flowing robes. He had long silver hair, a beard, and a true, kind, wizard's face. The only thing missing was a wizard's magic wand. The kindly looking wizard was holding up a sign that read:

"Help me! I'm imprisoned by the evil Wizard Shanevil. I'm the kindly Wizard Shagoodie. I need to escape and save the Teeny-taints from evil Shanevil."

There was nothing they could do except shrug their shoulders. They knew that helping the kindly wizard would bring them certain death from the evil Shanevil.

The Wizard cupped his hands around his mouth and lip-synced, "We'll be back to free you, Shagoodie. I promise."

Shagoodie, the kindly wizard, gave them a thumbs up, indicating he knew what the Wizard of Oz had said.

"He read my lips." The Wizard of Oz beamed. He peered over the side of the basket and was shocked by what he saw. The balloon was dropping like a stone.

"Rosebud, get down here now," the Wizard shouted. "I can see the ground below, and we're going to hit it hard. Hang on tight, everybody."

She scrambled down the ropes and scooped up Apricot, holding her close to protect her. Rosebud and the Wizard clung to the rim of the basket and hung on, awaiting the collision. Dee, having no hands, grabbed the rim of the basket with her teeth. She was dreading what might happen to her three good legs or her teeth when the basket hit the ground. *I'll never be able to eat grass again,* she thought.

They were in a freefall and would surely be killed when the basket struck the earth. Everyone was screaming and staring in fear at the fate that awaited them.

Thinking fast, the Wizard shouted, "You two, get over here by my side and help me sway this basket, and hopefully, we won't crash. Now, do as I do, rock left, then right. Good, keep it going. It's the only chance we have." Their weight made the basket sway back forth.

The swaying worked. The basket, instead of coming straight down and crashing, bounced off the top of a snow covered hill and began to glide down its side like a toboggan. They hit a buried rock at the foot of the hill and, "Thud, Boom, Bam!" The basket flipped over, throwing everyone into a huge pile of soft, multicolored, fluffy snow.

The Wizard, Rosebud, and Apricot were buried in the soft snow up to their necks. Dee had fallen into the snow pile so that only her butt and kicking back legs were visible.

"I'm okay, but is anyone hurt?" the Wizard asked.

"Not me," Rosebud assured him.

"I'm fine except for my sprained leg," said Dee, flipping around so her face stuck out of the snow.

"Meow!" answered Apricot, which in kitten meant, "Okay!" Rosebud and the Wizard dug themselves out of the snow, and Apricot jumped into Rosebud's arms.

They glanced at each other and began to laugh. Everyone was covered with multicolored snow and excited about being unhurt.

"Do you realize what an incredible ride we just took? And we're unhurt?" the Wizard asked.

"I sure do," agreed Dee.

"Me too," said Rosebud.

"It's a wonder we weren't all killed?" the Wizard said.

"It sure is," said Rosebud, gazing around. Her jaw dropped wide open at what she saw.

They were staring at several dollhouse-size, multicolored igloos.

"This is a strange place we've landed in. I wonder if anyone lives in those tiny igloos at the foot of that cliff?" Dee said.

"Or if they're friendly?" added Rosebud.

They stared at each other and at the igloos. No one was laughing anymore!

CHAPTER XII

A Doomed Teeny-Taints Village

"You're right, Dee. This is a strange place we've landed in! Let's get the balloon repaired and get out of here while we still can," the Wizard said, leading the way to the upside-down basket.

Rosebud was picking up their scattered goods. "I wonder how much damage was done to the basket when it flipped over?" she asked

They approached the basket and noticed that the deflated balloon was lying on top of it. A faint voice was heard pleading from underneath, "Help me! Help me! I can't get out from under this avalanche."

"Who's there?" the Wizard shouted, not knowing what to expect. "Maybe it's an evil Shanevil trick? Be careful, everyone," he warned.

"Are you friend or foe?" Dee demanded.

"Help me! Help me! I can't get out from under this avalanche," the faint voice repeated.

"Did I hear the word avalanche?" Dee asked, stepping away from the basket. "There wasn't any avalanche. Perhaps you're right, Wizard. Maybe it is an evil Shanevil trick?"

Again, the faint voice pleaded for help.

"Someone's trapped under the basket," Rosebud said.

The Wizard grabbed onto the deflated balloon. "Rosebud, help me pull the balloon off of the basket.

The two of them grabbed the balloon and pulled it off of the basket. When the balloon was out of the way, Dee pushed the basket with her antlers, turning it upright again.

"This is strange," Dee said. "There's no one in here!

Rosebud knelt on the snow-covered ground next to the pile of clothing and asked, "Is anyone under here?"

"Yes, there is. Help me out from under this avalanche," the muffled voice begged.

The Wizard lifted off the pile of clothing.

"Oh my goodness! Would you look at this!" A wide-eyed Rosebud stared in disbelief.

Sitting on the snow-covered ground was a little pot-bellied man. He was no more than six-inches tall. He was dressed in a brilliantly colored top hat, suit, shirt and tie. He wore tiny, matching multicolored socks and shoes on his itsy-bitsy feet. The little man stood up sputtering and spitting out snow.

"Who do we have here?" the Wizard asked.

"I'll tell you who you have here!" the little man roared. He approached the Wizard, madder than a sparrow after a chicken hawk.

"You have the one and only Crayon Tinge, mayor of the village of Teeny-taints. We have the smallest village and people in the world. But we don't tolerate being picked on." Mayor Tinge was hopping up and down like a monkey on a rubber tire.

"Wait a minute, Mayor Tinge," the Wizard said. "We're not here to hurt you, or any of your villagers. We fell out of the sky when our balloon lost its hot air, and we accidentally landed on top of you. We're hoping that you can help us repair the hole in our balloon. Then we can fill the balloon with hot air and fly away. Why are you so angry with us?"

"I'm not angry with you. It's the evil Shanevil that has me upset. He's our worst enemy and he has threatened to . . ." Mayor Tinge stopped in mid-sentence and broke into a friendly smile. He stared in amazement at Rosebud and Apricot. Then he walked over and stood next to Rosebud. "What have we here?" he asked looking up at her.

Rosebud was about eleven-inches taller than the mayor. Even though Mayor Tinge had his top hat on, Rosebud was able to see over his head. It was the first time in her life that she was taller than anyone else. "My name is Rosebud, and I'm very, very happy to meet you," she said with a polite curtsy and a sheepish grin.

"Wait until you meet my son Strawtop," Mayor Tinge said. You're going to love him. What a wonderful tiny cat! This must be your pet. He gave Apricot a friendly head rub. Mayor Tinge turned to Dee, "Why are you here and not in the air helping people and animals stranded in the snow?" he asked.

Dee told Mayor Tinge how she ended up in the basket with a sprained leg, unable to fly.

"It's too bad you can't fly, Dee. We could sure use your services right now." Mayor Tinge sighed. "What about you?" he asked the Wizard. "Who are you, big guy?"

"I'm the Wizard of Oz, and I'm in charge of this crew. It's my duty to get them to Kansas, wherever it is. Now let me ask you something, Mayor Tinge. Why were you pleading with us to get you out from under an avalanche when there was none?"

Mayor Tinge told them, "The evil wizard Shanevil is about to bury our village with an avalanche from that mountain high above us. The snow will roar down the side of the mountain, and we Teeny-taints, and now you and your crew will be killed by it. When your basket landed on top of me, I thought it was the avalanche. Fortunately, it was only your basket that knocked me down and almost killed me."

"Unfortunately, we didn't see you when we were sliding down the hill or we would have shouted a warning," the Wizard said.

"Well, that's water over the dam. I have a more important thing to worry about now. How am I going to save my villagers from the avalanche?" Mayor Tinge moaned.

"When is the evil Shanevil planning to bury your village, Mayor Tinge? And why?" the Wizard asked.

"We're a peace-loving people. In the winter, we make lots of toys, cookies, clothes, candies, and other items. In the summer, when the snow has melted, we climb to the top of this mountain and sell or trade our goods with the Unkies. Then we take the money and buy provisions and craft items to last us through the following winter."

"A few weeks ago," Mayor Tinge continued, "the evil Shanevil attempted to steal the crafts we made this past winter. It was his plan to sell them to the Unkies and keep the money. Had he been successful, we would have had nothing to trade for food this summer, and would have starved to death over the coming winter."

"Is there any way you can stop Shanevil, or talk him out of causing the avalanche?" Rosebud asked, wide-eyed with disbelief that someone would do such a dastardly deed.

"At one time we had a way to stop Shanevil, but now we don't," the mayor said.

"Why not?" Dee asked.

"Our guardian angel, the good wizard Shagoodie, found out about Shanevil's plan to steal our goods and stopped him before he could get away with it. Shanevil became very angry with Shagoodie for preventing the theft. He also got angry with us and has been causing nothing but trouble ever since. Shanevil will bury our village, and all of us with it, at high noon today."

"We saw your good wizard Shagoodie trapped in the ice prison on our way down," the Wizard said. "Our only chance is to round up everyone and get them out of danger before noon."

Dee added, "We have plenty of time to get away. It's only nine-thirty. That will give us two and a-half-hours to get to the high ground where we'll be safe. We can help you and your people escape from the village before noon."

"If we try to escape, and Shanevil sees us, he has promised to bring the avalanche down at that time. We are doomed, oh my, oh my!" Mayor Tinge paced in a circle, wondering what he could do to save his villagers.

By this time, the other Teeny-taints had heard the commotion, left their igloos, and gathered around their beloved, Mayor Tinge. Ironically, Mayor Tinge was a head taller than the rest of the Teeny-taints. They were each about five inches tall and dressed in the same colors as the mayor. The only difference between them was that Mayor Tinge wore a top hat and the other Teeny-taints wore stocking caps.

Rosebud was ecstatic. She felt like a giant standing among the Teeny-taints. She couldn't stop giggling. "How lovely your colors are! Why is everyone and everything multicolored?" she asked.

"Many years ago, everything here in the village was snow white," the mayor said. "When you live through nine months of winter each year, the white becomes depressing. We asked the good wizard Shagoodie to make us and our surroundings multicolored, and he sprinkled red, yellow, green, and blue tinted snow all over our village. Since then we've been very happy, because nothing is drab anymore. How ironic that we got rid of our depressing white snow, and now we're about to be buried forever under a pile of it." Mayor Tinge could only shake his head in disbelief.

The Wizard pointed toward a large building and asked, "How many Teeny-taints live in your village, and what is the purpose of that three-story, dome-roofed barn over there?"

"Sixty-three Teeny-taints are currently living here. The three-story building is our work and storage area. We keep it full of the crafts we produce. It's quite empty right now, because we sold everything to the Unkies. The only things left are the goods that we will use for next year's crafts."

Rosebud cried in frustration. "We only have a little over two hours before we get buried. Doesn't anyone have an idea of how we can escape this certain death?"

"I don't know about the rest of you, but I'm not ready to die," Dee said, pacing in a circle with the mayor. "There must be something we can do. What is it? Everyone think hard."

The Teeny-taints and Mayor Tinge shrugged their shoulders and shook their heads. They had thought of everything and couldn't come up with a way to escape their certain death. They were doomed. Everybody, including the children, looked sadly at the Wizard of Oz for an answer. But the Wizard could only shrug his shoulders and stare sadly back at them.

CHAPTER XIII

THE EVIL WIZARD OF DEATH AWAKENS

Mayor Tinge stopped pacing in a circle and put his hands behind his back. He began to pace back and forth, trying to come up with a plan. The Wizard put his hands behind his back and began to pace back and forth behind Mayor Tinge. Then Rosebud, with Apricot at her heels, paced behind the Wizard, and Dee paced behind Apricot.

The rest of the Teeny-taints put their hands behind their backs and paced back and forth behind Apricot. Together, they made a strange looking parade.

The Wizard came to a sudden stop, threw his hands in the air, pumped his fists, and proclaimed, "I have an escape plan!"

Those pacing behind the Wizard couldn't stop and bumped into his legs. Everyone, including the Wizard, toppled to the ground like dominoes. The only ones left standing were Mayor Tinge and Dee. This was because the mayor was leading the pacers and didn't get bumped into, and Dee's legs were so tall, she merely stepped over those who had fallen.

Mayor Tinge turned to ask the Wizard about his plan, and noticing everyone lying on the ground, he began to laugh and laugh. He laughed so hard that he too fell to the ground. Soon everyone was on the ground rolling with laughter.

"That laughter was fun. We Teeny-taints haven't laughed like that in a long time. It was just what we needed," a happy mayor said.

"Now back to business. What's your escape plan, Wizard?" Mayor Tinge was eager to find out.

"Do you have canvas, thread, and glue in your warehouse?" the Wizard asked.

"Yes, of course we do. We use nothing but the very finest of materials to make our goods. Why do you ask?"

"If we can find a piece of canvas large enough, we'll sew a patch on the balloon and fly out of here. My basket is large enough to hold your entire village of Teeny-taints, and altogether they don't weigh enough to prevent the balloon from getting into the air. So let's do it!" the Wizard said.

The Teeny-taints cheered the Wizard's escape plan.

"Gather your people, Mayor Tinge, and let's get started. We have no time to waste," the Wizard said, leading the way to the deflated balloon.

Mayor Tinge inspected the hole in the balloon. "The hole isn't that big. We can patch it with no problem.

Cutters, sewers, and gluers, grab your supplies from the warehouse, and let's get this balloon repaired."

The Teeny-taints were dashing to get the necessary supplies from the warehouse, when, "Kaboom," a huge, hot, bolt of lightning struck in the middle of the Town Square. They were all blown off of their feet and lay on the ground dazed, wondering what had happened.

A woman shrieked, pointed at the sky, and screamed, "It's the evil Shanevil!"

Hovering high above the Teeny-taints, taller than their three-story warehouse, was the evil Shanevil. He had awakened from his nap and was feeling ornery and ruthless. They could smell his pungent breath and feel the slime dripping from his nose as it fell on them. Angry fire and smoke was belching like a volcano from his hollow eye sockets. His pet rats and snakes were hissing, squealing, and weaving back and forth. They would thrust at the Teeny-taints, causing them to cower closer to the ground.

A rat the size of a pit bull, with giant fangs and bloody drool hanging from its foul-smelling mouth, leaped off of Shanevil's robe and landed in the middle of the Teeny-taints, who ran screaming in every direction. The rat cornered one of the Teeny-taints against a tree. But before the rat could devour him, a snake longer than a bus, with fangs larger than elephant tusks, swooped out of Shanevil's robe pocket. The snake stared directly into the terrified eyes of the rat. Before the rat could move, the snake struck with the speed of a comet and instantly devoured it. The rat was still kicking as it went down the snake's throat and into its belly. The snake stared at the Teeny-taints like they were next. Luckily, it only hissed and returned to Shanevil's pocket.

Shanevil roared, "No one can escape the death I have planned for you today. If you attempt to flee again, I will send a bolt of lightning and fry you like eggs. Then I'll eat you for a snack or feed you to my rats and snakes. Perhaps I should bury you now." "Kaboom!" The evil Shanevil sent another bolt of lightning into the Town Square. It hit so close that it singed their eyebrows and the hair on their bodies. Some even had the lens in their eyeglasses start to melt.

"Watch the mayor's igloo." Shanevil sneered. He sent a bolt of lightning and blew the igloo into several thousand multicolored ice cubes.

"Hurry, everyone, follow me before Shanevil sends another bolt of lightning," Mayor Tinge shouted, leading the way into the giant warehouse. "If Shanevil doesn't kill us, the avalanche will. We're doomed if we do, and doomed if we don't."

Everyone was in the warehouse sobbing and shaking with fear. Rosebud was looking around to see what she could do to help. "I found a huge pile of multicolored canvas. We can sew it into a new balloon, attach it to the silver basket, and fly out of here," she yelled.

"That's it, Rosebud! You've solved our problem!" the Wizard said. "We can make the new balloon here in the warehouse without evil Shanevil seeing us. Not only that, the domed roof of the warehouse is so high that we can make our new balloon twice the size of the old one. We'll be able to fly out of here without any fear of being overloaded."

The Wizard drew a pattern for the new balloon and gave it to the cutters, sewers, and gluers. "Hurry," he said. "It's only one hour until noon."

Dee and the Wizard gathered a crew and led them to the silver basket.

"Here's my plan," the Wizard said. Detach the balloon from the basket, spread it out, and leave it lying on the ground. Let's hope that Shanevil sees it and believes that we are not going to attempt an escape After all, how can we fly without a balloon?"

After detaching the balloon, the crew picked up the basket and carried it into the warehouse. The Wizard's plan had worked, and no one got fried or eaten like an egg.

The Teeny-taints finished making the new balloon, and attached it to the basket.

"I need everyone to practice getting into the basket, and hurry!" the Wizard ordered. "Now that you're in the basket, here's what I need you to do. Everyone spread out and sit so the load will be evenly distributed. By doing this, the basket is less likely to tip on its side and throw you out. Please remember your spot for later."

The Teeny-taints left the basket, and the Wizard began filling the balloon with hot air. The balloon grew larger and larger until it was completely filled and pressing hard against the domed ceiling of the warehouse.

"Wow!" Mayor Tinge said, "I've never seen anything bigger or prettier in my entire life! But how are we going to get out of the warehouse with the roof attached to it? We can't fly through it, can we? And what are we going to do about the evil Shanevil? If he sees us taking the roof off, and the new balloon inside of it, he's going to hit us with a bolt of lightning, and that will be the end. Oh dear, oh dear," Mayor Tinge moaned in dismay.

"Mayor, don't you or any of you other Teeny-taints worry about the evil Shanevil finding out what we're doing. I've got this whole thing figured out—I think." The Wizard gulped.

CHAPTER XIV

A DEADLY AVALANCHE

"What do you think you've got figured out, Wizard?" Dee asked.

"I know how we can get out of the warehouse and past the evil Shanevil,"

"Wizard, how can you possibly get through that thick roof? Do you think your balloon's a giant circular saw?" Mayor Tinge teased.

"An avalanche stays close to the side of a mountain. When it hits high speeds, it pushes hurricane winds and tons of snow ahead of it. The snow flies into the air and forms a cloud several miles high. When the avalanche reaches the bottom of this mountain, its hurricane winds will blow the roof off of this giant warehouse like it was a seeding dandelion."

"Then what?" an anxious Rosebud wanted to know.

"The winds will lift us out of the warehouse, and we'll ride the white snow cloud out of here without being seen by the evil Shanevil. But, in order not to be seen, we need to blend in with the snow cloud. Everyone grab a pail of white paint and your spray painters, and start painting everything on this vessel white. Hurry, it's almost noon!" the Wizard said, checking his watch.

The Teeny-taints grabbed a brush or spray painter and quickly painted the balloon, basket, and ropes. No sooner had they finished painting when Mayor Tinge's son, Strawtop (named for his brownish colored hair), came rushing into the warehouse. Strawtop had been out searching for an escape route, and after returning to the village, he discovered the deflated balloon in the Village Square.

"There's trouble outside, we need to . . ." But before he could finish speaking, Strawtop saw the huge balloon touching the ceiling.

"Well, I'll be!" He laughed.

Rosebud had never seen anyone like Strawtop. He was very young and handsome with baby blue eyes, brownish hair, and a body that looked like he had been pumping iron forever. Strawtop was dressed in tight-fitting blue jeans, a red designer shirt, a tan vest and belt, with matching tan leather boots. To make everything perfect, he was only twenty inches tall.

Rosebud thought of what her mother would say to her when she was depressed, '*Don't give up! Somewhere out there is a boy your size looking for someone your size.*' Now they had found each other. It was love at first sight.

"Hi, my name's Rosebud. I never thought I would find a handsome boy my size. I couldn't be happier than I am at this moment," she said with a blush and a curtsy.

"My name's Embl, but everyone calls me Strawtop. I too have never been happier. I never thought I would find a girl my size, especially one so pretty. Too bad we are going to be buried by a landslide in a few minutes," Strawtop said, holding Rosebud's hand. "I tried desperately to find an escape route, but it was no use."

"We've found a way for everyone to escape in this giant balloon," Rosebud said. And then she explained their plan.

"Hey, you two, there's no time for talking. We've got work to do if we're going to escape Shanevil and his deadly avalanche," the Wizard warned.

The Wizard realized that to make his plan succeed he had to be certain the roof would blow off when it got hit with the hurricane winds.

"I need everyone to climb up those ladders set along the wall and remove the nails holding down the domed roof. With the nails removed, the roof should blow off when the wind hits it. Then we'll be lifted like a rocket, straight up into the air for several miles. The evil Shanevil will think his avalanche has buried us forever and, if it works, he'll never bother us again. Now hurry, we have only ten minutes until noon."

No sooner had the nails been pulled from the roof when, "Kaboom!" A mighty bolt of lightning struck the gigantic ridge of snow and loosened it from the top of the mountain. From high above they heard a loud, evil Shanevil laugh followed by a low rumble. The deadly avalanche was on its way, and nothing could stop it now. The loosened snow began to move slowly down the side of the mountain. It didn't take long before the avalanche had gained incredible speed and was roaring down on them like a runaway freight train. The ground under the basket began to shake like it was standing on a giant bowl of jelly.

The powerful avalanche was swallowing up everything in its path as it roared toward the warehouse. Rocks, trees, and buildings were caught up in its powerful path of destruction. Fear had gripped everyone. Was this the end?

CHAPTER XV

WHAT IF?

"Everybody, get into the basket and take your places, now!" the Wizard shouted above the roar of the oncoming avalanche.

They scrambled madly into the basket, as they had done during practice. Each person went immediately to his or her assigned place. They interlocked arms and legs so they wouldn't be blown away by the gale force winds. Everybody prayed that they would make it out alive. "I love you," was heard all around.

Rosebud held Apricot close to give her comfort in this time of great peril. Strawtop sat next to Rosebud with one arm around her, his other arm clutching firmly to the basket. It had taken years for him to find his true love and he wasn't about to lose her now. Or was he?

The Wizard and Dee stood over the Teeny-taints to protect them from the debris that would soon be flying all around them. The Wizard's biggest fear was that a piece of the debris would hit the balloon and deflate it before they could rise above the avalanche. If this happened, they would perish instantly.

"What if the roof doesn't blow off? What do we do then?" Mayor Tinge screamed at the Wizard.

"What if the roof blows off and we don't rise fast enough to escape the avalanche?" Strawtop hollered.

"We'll know the answer in a few seconds," the Wizard shouted. He was desperately trying to yell above the roar of the nightmare that was about to engulf them. It was the kind of nightmare that one might never wake up from.

The Wizard watched the roof above him shaking violently up and down. "Break loose, break loose, break loose, and fly away. Go, roof, go!" the Wizard screamed. He was waving his arms up and down in an effort to lift the roof off of its walls.

"Dee," the Wizard yelled, "we're about to be buried here forever or lifted out like a rocket going to the moon. Lock your head in the crook of my arm so you can take the pressure off your bad leg. I'll hang on to you as best I can. If we go, we'll go together."

Those were the last words the Wizard would get a chance to say. The avalanche had now roared down upon the village. In an instant, the igloos were buried under thousands of tons of snow, rocks, and trees. The avalanche hit the ground and headed, full force, directly at the warehouse and its terrified occupants. "Go, roof, go!" they screamed!

The door to the warehouse was blown out before Dee could put her head in the crook of the Wizard's arms. Without the door, they were hit by a blast of cold, snowy wind. The wind was so powerful that it almost knocked both of them off of their feet. It was a wind, the force of which, none in the basket had ever experienced before. At the same time, the domed warehouse roof ripped loose and was lifted fifty feet into the air. It was spinning like a top, making it look like a giant UFO. The roof momentarily lingered high above the warehouse before it plummeted straight down toward them. It would surely crush the balloon and bring certain death to all.

Everyone covered their heads with their hands and began crying hysterically. However, before the roof could crush them, a powerful wind shear struck the walls of the warehouse, ripping them from their foundations and blowing them away like they were so much dust.

The powerful wind hit the balloon with such force that it was instantly blown sideways. Another second and they would have been crushed by the falling roof. The balloon and its terrified passengers were sent rocketing toward the top of the mountain high above. It rose so fast that they were slammed to the floor and rolled around like pool balls. They looked like a pile of discarded dolls that you might find in a large department store at Christmas time. Then, the balloon was struck by a giant snowball and spun up and down and all around. The basket was spinning faster than a top. It was like a terrifying ride at a State Fair. Fortunately, none of the panic stricken occupants were injured, or lost overboard. Or were they?

The balloon rode the crest of the wind up the side of the mountain, speeding like a high-balling roller coaster. Then, for an instant, the wind went silent as the balloon passed the ice castle. The Wizard of Oz was able to see that the evil Shanevil was trapped in a clear glass gallon jug. Evil Shanevil's vile face was pressed hard against the inside of the jug, and he was screaming for help. The good wizard Shagoodie was holding the jug high and cheering them on. The Wizard gave Shagoodie two thumbs up. He had no idea how evil Shanevil wound up in the glass jug, but he was very relieved that he had. Then the balloon again rocketed upward toward the mountain top.

Quicker than you could bat an eye, the balloon was high above the top of the mountain. It slowed its ascent when a friendly gust of wind blew it north.

"We did it!" a triumphant Wizard shouted, raising his hands high. Everyone including the Wizard was covered in snow. He got up from his knees and spoke to those who were lying on the floor. "Is everyone okay?" he asked, helping them to brush off the snow and get to their feet.

"Let's do it again, Wizard! That was fun!" One of the children giggled.

Everyone was laughing over their fabulous ride and the fact that they were at last free of the evil Shanevil.

Rosebud rose to her feet and grasped the Wizard's hand. She was sobbing uncontrollably.

"Apricot and Dee are gone!" Rosebud cried. "The blast of wind that hit us caused me to lose my grip on Apricot, and the wind blew her away. Dee saw

Apricot fly out of my arms and jumped after her. The two of them are buried forever in the rubble far below. "They're gone! They're gone! And they're never coming back." Rosebud sobbed.

"Dee was a hero. She bravely gave her life trying to save another," Mayor Tinge said, turning his head so no one would see him wiping away a tear. He turned to hide another tear and noticed, through the floor's basket weave, that something was hanging from a mooring rope. "Oh my goodness, look at this! I can't believe it!" He dropped down on all fours to get a better view.

The others dropped down to look through the floor of the basket, and there, dangling from a mooring rope held tightly in her teeth, was Dee. She was biting on the rope so hard that you could see every blood vessel in her face. She was swinging back and forth like a pendulum on a grandfather clock.

"Apricot is holding tight to Dee's tail," Strawtop said, his voice filled with relief and joy.

"Quick, help me pull them in," Rosebud said. She was happy beyond words as she tugged with all her might on the mooring rope.

Everyone grabbed a piece of the mooring rope and pulled Dee and Apricot into the basket. The two of them were covered with snow from head to toe, and they were half frozen. They rubbed and brushed the snow off Dee and Apricot and covered them with blankets to warm them up.

"Thank you, Dee, thank you, thank you," Rosebud said over and over. She nestled Apricot close in her lap to warm her up. Apricot purred with delight.

Dee was busy thanking everyone for rescuing them.

"Our ride to the top was terrifying," a shivering Dee said. "At one time the balloon and basket were spinning over and over. One moment we were hanging below the basket, and the next we were flipped upside down. Then it went into a spin and I thought I was going to be sick. In fact, it spun so fast that all of the white paint on the rope peeled off. Fortunately, we hit a dead space in the wind and momentarily stopped spinning. Otherwise I don't believe we would have survived.

"It was terribly cold in that white cloud. I couldn't see a thing until we passed over the mountain top and headed north. I would have had to let go of the rope with my teeth to holler for help. Worse yet, I couldn't let my teeth chatter, or I would have lost my grip on the rope, or maybe even bit it in half. Can we fly to someplace warm?" Dee pleaded.

"Yes, let's fly to someplace warm," the others agreed.

"I have no control over this balloon, or where it goes," the Wizard said. "Unfortunately, the only place we can go is wherever the wind blows us. Rosebud and I are trying to get to Kansas, and we have no idea where it is. The one thing I know for sure is that we're heading north, and I don't think that's the direction we need to travel to get to a warm climate, or to Kansas. However, everyone's safe, and we can be thankful for that."

"We certainly are thankful," Mayor Tinge agreed. "Dee, do you have any idea where we are?"

"I don't have a clue. We may get some idea of our location when we clear the Alps in the morning. If I could fly, I might be able to find Kansas. Then you could harness me to one of the tethering ropes, and I could tow you there. The problem is, as usual, I might get lost trying to find Kansas and will never come back to you."

"No way!" Rosebud said. "If you can't find us again, you may wind up crashing or perhaps hurt one of your other legs, or maybe . . ."

Rosebud covered her mouth with both hands and went mum.

"If only I could fly and find my way like the other reindeer in my squadron. How wonderful that would be!" Dee said.

"If I had become taller, like I always wanted to, I would be very unhappy right now," Rosebud said, squeezing Strawtop's hand.

"If I were shorter, like I always wanted to be, I would be very unhappy," Strawtop said, winking at Rosebud.

"Well," the Wizard said, "it seems to me that everyone, with the exception of Dee, wanted to be or do something they couldn't, and now they can. Perhaps, before our journey's end, I can do something to help Dee find her way back no matter where she goes. Then she can finally finish her training. But we've got to fly to Kansas first."

They continued on in a northerly direction, the weather getting colder. Would the wind change direction and blow them to the sunny, warm climate they longed for, or did some other fate await them?

The Wizard thought, *"Why are we constantly being driven north? Is Kansas over the next mountain top? If not, what is?*

CHAPTER XVI

THE PURPLE PICKAPLUMS

The morning sun was casting long shadows on the valleys far below. The balloon and its passengers were about to pass over the last Alp mountain. It had been a long, dangerous trek across the Alps, and the Wizard and Rosebud were very glad to be away from them. Ahead, as far as they could see, lay a vast, barren, snow and sun-covered plain.

"Rosebud," the Wizard said, "That plain we're about to cross appears to be endless. It seems that we have a long, long trip to go yet. I don't see anything out there that's gray-colored like Kansas. Do you?"

"You're right, Wizard. I don't see anything that looks like Kansas either. Do you think we'll ever find it?" Rosebud sighed.

Strawtop shouted from his perch on top of the basket. "I see a strange purple village at the base of the high Alp we just passed over."

"Strawtop," the Wizard asked, "is that a purple sign I see below us?"

"It's definitely a sign, but I can't read it. We're too far away."

"Let's drop down and see what the sign says. Maybe they're giving away a free hot breakfast," Mayor Tinge joked.

"Yes," they all agreed.

"A hot breakfast would taste great, free or not," Rosebud said, rubbing her stomach.

The Wizard grabbed a cord and released some hot air from the balloon. They descended toward the unknown purple village and an uncertain fate.

When they dropped close enough to the sign, Strawtop was able to read it. "The purple sign says, 'Help us save Cloudine!'" he said.

"Here we go again." Dee sighed.

The Wizard stopped letting the hot air escape from the balloon to keep it from dropping any closer to the ground. "What do you make of the sign?" he asked Mayor Tinge

"Perhaps it's another evil wizard trying to lure us into a trap, or worse, maybe Shanevil has escaped from the glass jug, and he's playing a fateful game! Let's fly out of here before we get into more trouble." Mayor Tinge had a note of fear in his voice.

"I wouldn't worry about Shanevil," the Wizard said. "I don't believe he'll ever escape from the glass jug or the good wizard Shagoodie. Besides, if it were Shanevil, he would have hit us with a bolt of lightning by now."

Rosebud asked, "Is that a purple dressed lady that I see waving her arms back and forth and shouting something that I can't understand. Did anyone hear it?"

The person stopped waving and cupping her mouth, again shouted something at the balloon. Only Dee could hear what the person was shouting. Her hearing was trained for emergency situations such as this.

"Wizard," Dee said. "She isn't waving hello to us, she's asking for our help. I think we should drop down and see what we can do to help her."

"I agree with Dee," Mayor Tinge said.

"I'm with both of you," the Wizard said. He again pulled the cord and gradually let some of the hot air out of the balloon. It was his plan to land on the sun-covered frozen plain far enough away from the stranger so they could easily escape if necessary.

They landed close to the purple village and noticed that the purple lady, who was calling and waving to them, was wearing a purple hat and scarf, a purple coat and muffler, and a purple gown and boots.

"Do you think the purple dressed lady is real, or a robot?" Rosebud asked.

"I'll find out," the Wizard said. "But to be safe, everyone stay in the basket. If it is the evil Shanevil, I'll wave my arms. Mayor, when you see me waving my arms, tug this white rope and the balloon will fill with hot air. Then you can fly away from here. I have shown Rosebud and Strawtop how to control the balloon, and they'll fly you to safety."

"What if that purple lady is Shanevil in disguise? Won't he blast us out of the air before we can fly away?" Strawtop asked.

"Yes, he will," the Wizard replied. He stepped out of the basket and walked toward the purple village and the purple lady. Everyone stared at each other in disbelief.

"Wizard, I'm going with you in case you run into trouble!" Dee said.

"Okay, Dee, come on." The wizard was grateful to have Dee's company.

Dee stepped out of the basket and joined the Wizard. She was limping noticeably.

The Wizard and Dee were halfway to the village when they stopped in their tracks and stared in awe.

"Do you see what I see?" Dee asked in amazement.

"I think I do," the Wizard said, rubbing his eyes in disbelief. "Is that purple 'Help us free Cloudine' sign walking this way?"

"Indeed it is," the laughing purple 'Help us save Cloudine' sign said. "We're the people known as the Pickaplums. And this is our purple village, also called Pickaplums. We're very happy that you came to help us rescue our friend Cloudine from the frozen plain."

"I'm the Wizard of Oz, and this is my friend Dee, the flying reindeer. Are you glued to each other?" The Wizard gazed in disbelief.

"No, we just wrap our arms around each other to make signs!" The Pickaplums laughed. Then they opened their arms and separated from one another.

"They're children." Dee giggled in delight.

The children had ceramic, painted-white doll faces. Their faces looked like they would shatter if they fell and hit them on the frozen ground. Each of them had sky blue eyes, long black eyelashes, black eyebrows, apple red lips, and cherry pink cheeks and noses. The rest of their bodies were purple. They wore purple snowsuits, boots, and mittens.

"Who are you?" the Wizard asked, bowing to the tallest one.

"I'm the Princess Magenta, the one who waved and shouted at you."

Princess Magenta was the most beautiful lady the Wizard had ever seen. She had delicate features, jet black eyes, and white flawless skin smoother than the finest silk. When the princess spoke, the air became still as a pond at midnight. Every word she uttered cast a magical spell on the Wizard. The princess stood straight and tall like an elegant long-stemmed rose.

Taken aback by her great beauty, the Wizard, for the first time in his life, was at a loss for words.

Princess Magenta, was likewise enchanted by the Wizard, whose bravery and wisdom had become legendary in the Alps. When their eyes met, it was love at first glance for the two of them.

"Who are these children? And who are you, beautiful princess?" Dee asked.

"These are the children of the village of Pickaplums. Their parents allowed them to lie out here in the snow and form the 'Help us save Cloudine' sign. We knew that when the wonderful Wizard of Oz saw our sign, he would come and help us rescue a friend in need. And here you are!"

"And I'm very glad to be here, Princess," the Wizard said with a bow. "Now what can we do to help you and your friend Cloudine?"

"Our friend Cloudine is stuck in the middle of that huge snowball at the edge of the village. Because you are a magical wizard, we know that with your help we can free her. You will help us, won't you?" she pleaded.

"Princess Magenta, who is Cloudine, and why can't you get her out of the snowball?" the Wizard asked. He avoided any reference to being a magical wizard.

"Cloudine is our snow woman friend. We can't tell where she begins and ends in the snowball. We're afraid that if we try to release her, and fail, we might split her in two, or worse yet, crunch her into pieces. If that happens, she'll be trapped in the snowball forever!

"She's known throughout the Alps for her entertaining ways and generosity. Cloudine can sing, dance, yodel, perform magic, and do lots of other fun things. She travels around the Alps babysitting, working in schools, and hosting children's parties.

"Last night she was entertaining at a children's birthday party on top of this mountain and she got carried away. Now she's inside the giant snowball," the princess cried.

"What do you mean, she got carried away?" the Wizard wanted to know.

"Call your friends in the white basket and follow me. We're going to my castle for hot chocolate, tea, and some of my homemade goodies. I'll explain everything when we get there," Princess Magenta said.

The Wizard signaled for everyone to come and join them. They followed Princess Magenta to her purple castle to learn about a friendly snow woman known as Cloudine.

CHAPTER XVII

ONE GIANT SNOWBALL ON THE WAY

Princess Magenta led the way into the kitchen of her purple castle. The kitchen was her pride and joy, and all were amazed and amused by what they saw.

The kitchen had long counters that were covered with various pies, cookies, muffins, stews, and soups— each one having its own pleasant, distinctive aroma and taste. The Wizard was very impressed that Princess Magenta had prepared these foods. "Grab your favorite goodies and drinks and follow me," the princess said.

"I have to marry this princess," the Wizard whispered to Rosebud.

The group followed the princess to her elegant dining room and marveled at the various shades of reds and pinks. Then she led them to the adjoining living room, decorated in brilliant shades of green. It was the living room where the princess invited them to be seated.

"Sit by the fireplace. It's warm and cozy."

Everyone gathered near the fireplace with their drinks and goodies and anxiously waited to hear the story of Cloudine.

They sat quietly and listened to Princess Magenta's fascinating tale.

"Many years ago, an American expedition climbed to the top of Mount Everest in the Himalayan Mountains. It's the highest mountain in the world. Before coming down the mountain, the expedition made a snow woman with a smiling face and, because they were high in the clouds, they called her, Cloudine."

"But if Cloudine was left on top of Mount Everest, how did she get here in the Alps?" Rosebud asked.

"Be patient," Princess Magenta said. "I'm getting to that." Then she continued.

"Cloudine stood on top of Mount Everest for fifty years watching over the world. She knew that she couldn't always make the world safe, but, with her happy face, she could always make it smile. The only time Cloudine saw anyone was when expeditions arrived, or airplanes went whizzing overhead. The expedition members would have their pictures taken with her and then go home. When expeditions did arrive, Cloudine was very happy, but when they left, she would be very lonely and unhappy. She longed to be with lots of people, especially children. Cloudine was so terribly lonely that her smiling face eventually turned into a frown.

"One day, another American expedition climbed to the top of Mount Everest. They stood next to Cloudine and had their pictures taken. One of the members of the expedition pulled out a picture of his father and Cloudine that had been taken fifty years before.

"'Look at this picture!' the climber said. 'Cloudine was smiling in my dad's picture and now she's frowning. Maybe she's been here too long! Let's take her away from here and relocate her!'

"For the first time in many years, Cloudine broke into a big smile. 'Yes,' another climber said, 'Cloudine smiled when you said she's been up here too long. But how do we get her out of here? She's much too heavy for us to carry down the mountain. If we accidently drop her on the way down, she'll smash into a million pieces and that will be the end of her.'

"'Not if we put Cloudine in our canteens!' climber number one said. 'We can melt her into water, pour her into our canteens, and rebuild her when we get back to the foot of the mountain.'

"They each agreed that this was a terrific idea. So they built a fire, melted Cloudine into water, and poured her into their canteens. Then they made another snow woman with a big smile on her face and put her in Cloudine's place."

"How did the expedition rebuild Cloudine when they got to the foot of Mount Everest?" Strawtop asked.

"And how did she get here in the Alps?" Mayor Tinge said.

"That's the amazing part of this whole story, Mayor Tinge," Princess Magenta continued. "When the members of the expedition arrived at the foot of Mount Everest, they realized that the weather was much too warm to rebuild Cloudine on that spot. They had to take her to a place where it was cold enough for her to survive. It had to be a place where she would wear a smiling face forever. The team knew that Cloudine had to be where there were lots of children to entertain. The obvious solution to the problem: rebuild Cloudine in the Alps."

"Then what happened?" Dee asked.

"They put the canteens with Cloudine in them on a plane and flew her to a ski area above our village. When they arrived at the ski area, they poured the contents of the canteens into a large snowmaking machine, turned it on, and out she blew, smiling and happy. Since that day, Cloudine has spent her time wandering through the Alps, entertaining children, and having fun."

"How did Cloudine get out on the sun-drenched, frozen plain?" Strawtop asked.

"Cloudine was entertaining at a child's birthday party yesterday. She was on top of this Alp high above us. Cloudine was leading the children on a parade through the village, when she came to a huge tree that had fallen over the trail. She got a little rambunctious and decided to jump over the tree instead of going around it. That was a big mistake!"

"Big mistake? What kind of a big mistake can a snow woman make?" Rosebud asked.

"When Cloudine attempted to jump over the fallen tree, she caught her feet on a branch, tripped, landed on a sheet of ice, and began to roll down the mountain before anyone could stop her. By the time she rolled to the edge of our village, she was completely encased in a perfectly round, huge snowball. We need to get Cloudine out of the snowball right away or we may never get her out! Do you think you can free Cloudine, oh great Wizard of Oz?"

"We need to go and study the snowball. Maybe then we can come up with an idea to save your friend Cloudine," Dee suggested to the group.

"Good idea! Let's do it!" Princess Magenta said, leading the way to Cloudine.

Chapter XVIII

Knock, Knock! Who's There?

Princess Magenta guided the Wizard and the other rescuers to the frozen snowball. "Here we are," she said.

Rosebuds eyes were aglow. "I've never seen a snowball this big. What did you mean when you said that Cloudine would be entombed in the giant snowball forever?" she asked.

Princess Magenta explained. "The spring sun is very warm today. Unfortunately, it is so warm that it will soon turn the outside of the snowball to mush. Tonight, cold, freezing air will sweep down from the mountains and across the plain. When this happens, the mush surrounding the snowball will freeze into a sheet of ice too thick to break apart. Cloudine will then be entombed in the giant snowball forever."

"Won't the sun melt the ice again tomorrow?" Mayor Tinge asked.

"The ice will be so thick by morning it can only partially melt during the warm day. Then when tomorrow night's freezing winds hit it, the ice will be twice the thickness as the previous day. Therefore, we must free Cloudine today, or never." Princess Magenta sobbed.

"I have an idea to save Cloudine," Rosebud stated.

"What is it?" the anxious princess asked.

"Let's bring our balloon to the giant snowball and use it for shade. That way it won't melt so fast. This will give us more time to come up with a plan to free Cloudine."

"We can't fly the balloon to the snowball unless the wind is blowing toward it, and right now it's not," the Wizard said.

"If we had enough people, we could pull the balloon to the snowball. However, this is all the people we have, and there's not enough time to send for help from a neighboring village," the princess said.

Dee spoke up. "I have the strength of ten men. My hooves are made to dig into the ice on this frozen plain. If you make a harness you can attach it to the basket and, with everyone's help we'll pull the balloon to the giant snowball in no time."

"That's a wonderful plan, Dee. Let's get started," the Wizard said, leading the way to the balloon. Princess Magenta walked proudly by his side.

"Dee, is your injured leg healed enough for you pull the balloon?" Rosebud asked.

"Rosebud, this is my first big mission, and I must succeed with it. If I do, the academy and its members will be very proud of me, for I will have helped to save a life. I have been sworn to perform my duties to the best of my ability, and I cannot let anything stop me, not even an injured leg." Dee marched gallantly to the balloon.

They arrived at the balloon, and the Wizard made a harness of heavy-duty rope and tied it around Dee's body. Then he tied the mooring ropes to Dee's harness. The Pickaplums, Strawtop, Rosebud, and Apricot, being very small, were placed in the basket with the Wizard for ballast and safekeeping. The others grabbed onto the mooring ropes and, with Dee's help, started towing the balloon to the giant snowball. The day was getting warmer and they had to hurry.

Dee pulled like she had never done before. At times a small gust of wind would push the balloon back and she had to work twice as hard to bring it to the snowball. But Dee refused to give up. She thought that she would collapse from the strain. Dee somehow found the courage and strength to go on. Then, to the cheers of the Pickaplums, she gave a final tug and was standing next to the giant snowball with the balloon at her side. Dee gave everyone a knowing smile and fell on her side, too tired to take another step.

Rosebud rushed to Dee's side and gave her water and a friendly pat on the head. "You're our hero!" she said.

"This snowball is bigger than I thought," the Wizard said. "Let's move the balloon around and see if we can block the sun." They did it and had enough shadow to cover the snowball from top to bottom.

The princess gave them directions. "Everyone, walk around the snowball and across the top. See if you can find a crack large enough to pop it open and free Cloudine."

Not one crack could be found. The snowball was perfectly smooth. It didn't even have a slight break in it.

"It's too bad we can't pick up the snowball and crack it like an egg," Strawtop said.

"That's it, Strawtop!" the Wizard said. "Why didn't I think of that before? We'll dig a ditch around the middle of the snowball. Then we'll tie it to the basket, lift it into the air, and drop it on the frozen plain. It will split it in half and out will walk Cloudine."

"Wizard, how can we Pickaplums help?" Princess Magenta asked. She too felt the excitement in the air.

"Send your people to the village and have them bring as many picks and shovels as they can carry. And hurry!" the Wizard told her.

"How do you know Cloudine won't be smashed to pieces when the snowball splits in half?" Rosebud asked.

"That's a chance we'll have to take if we're going to free Cloudine," the princess said. "I know what I'll do," she said. "I'll have my water well digger, Aqua Pira, drill a hole down to Cloudine. Then we can ask her if she agrees with our plan."

"That's fine," Strawtop said from the basket. "But how will you hear Cloudine's reply? Remember that she's most likely buried deep inside the snowball."

"You children, run to the village and get Aqua Pira and Doctor Gottazaminya," ordered Princess Magenta. When Aqua Pira reaches Cloudine with his equipment, he can ask her questions. Doctor Gottazaminya can hold his stethoscope against the side of the snowball, and tell us what Cloudine's replies are."

The children found Aqua Pira at the skating rink, smoothing the ice with his Zamboni. They informed him of the problem with Cloudine and that Princess Magenta was asking him to hurry and help save the snow woman. To get to the princess more quickly, Aqua Pira rode his Zamboni to the giant snowball.

Aqua Pira was a funny looking man. His limbs and hands appeared to be made out of water pipes. He wore a big cowboy hat that fell over his ears. The only things visible were his eyes, nose, and mouth. Aqua Pira was constantly drinking water from an old World War One canteen. He wore big baggy pants full of water testing equipment. Around his waist hung a huge tool belt containing, wrenches, drills, telescoping pipe, and other equipment needed to drill a well.

After sending Aqua Pira on his way, the children ran to find Doctor Gottazaminya. They found him in his office preparing medicines for the next day's house calls. When they informed him of the problem, he immediately fetched his black bag, jumped on his ragged old horse, and followed the Zamboni to the giant snowball.

Doctor Gottazaminya was a loving old doctor. He treated everyone who lived in the Alp Mountains. His gold spectacles were always on the tip of his bulbous nose. Doctor Gottazaminya had a face as wrinkled as a crumpled up old newspaper. He had long gray hair, a round bushy gray beard, and a gray oversized moustache. The good doctor wore a blue wool suit that needed a good pressing, and a wrinkled white shirt. Around his neck was a tie that contained a sample of every meal he had ever eaten. He had made so many house calls that his ragged old horse never had its saddle taken off. The horse always knew the way home while the doctor slept.

Princess Magenta told Aqua Pira and Doctor Gottazaminya what she wanted them to do, and they immediately went to work.

Aqua Pira took a large drill out of his tool belt and said to Doctor Gottazaminya, "I'm going to run this drill deep into the snowball. Then I will take this telescoping pipe and feed it down to Cloudine." With that, Aqua Pira used a wrench to grip the pipe. "I have to screw the pipe carefully and slowly toward the center of the giant snowball," he said, "or I might run the pipe into Cloudine and put a hole in her."

"I'll press my stethoscope against the snowball. That way, I can hear if your pipe accidentally hits Cloudine and makes her cry out in pain," Doctor Gottazaminya said.

When Aqua Pira had fed his pipe halfway through the snowball, he stopped drilling. Then he turned to Doctor Gottazaminya. "I'm going to try to talk with Cloudine by shouting through this pipe. Let me know if you hear her reply, and tell me what she says."

Aqua Pira put his mouth to the pipe and shouted, "Cloudine, this is Aqua Pira. If you can hear me, let me know." Aqua Pira took the pipe from his mouth and put it to his ear.

"I didn't hear anything, Doctor. Did you?" Aqua Pira asked.

"I sure did! Cloudine said she can hear you."

After determining that Cloudine was doing fine, Aqua Pira told her of their plan and cautioned her of the dangers. "Do you want us to go ahead?" he asked Cloudine.

Doctor Gottazaminya smiled and said, "Cloudine's feeling fine and said that you should go ahead with your plan to split the snowball in half. She also said that she was doing a funny skit for the children's party and still has her topcoat, long scarf, and top hat on. Apparently, her clothing twisted around her when she started rolling down the mountain, so she's wrapped up like a mummy. Cloudine says that with the clothing wrapped around her, she'll roll out of the snowball unharmed when it splits open."

The Pickaplums had returned with the picks and shovels. Princess Magenta said, "Everyone go to a spot on the middle of the snowball and spread out, pick, shovel, pick, shovel, and so on. I need you to dig a ditch one foot deep, and one foot wide, and be quick."

They dug and picked and soon had completed the ditch.

"Good job," the Wizard said. "Now let's remove the harness and ropes from Dee and use them to secure the snowball to the basket. I'll rig the ropes so that when the snowball is lifted high enough, at my command, a single pull on one of the ropes will send it crashing onto the frozen plain. Then, it will split in half and out will walk Cloudine. At least that's the plan."

"Now, it will be the mayor's job to control the balloon and Strawtop's job to pull the release rope when I give the command."

"Fire up the fuel tanks and let's get Cloudine out of the snowball," the Wizard shouted to Mayor Tinge. The princess and the Pickaplums began to clap their hands in excitement.

Mayor Tinge fired up the fuel tanks and filled the balloon with hot air. But try as they might, they could not get the snowball to budge. The base of it was frozen solidly to the plain.

"Everyone bring your picks and shovels and come over to this side of the snowball," the Wizard ordered.

They grabbed their picks and shovels and hurried to the Wizard's side.

"I want you Pickaplums to dig your picks and shovels into the base of the snowball right here by my foot. When the mayor has refilled the balloon, I'll give you a signal. Then I want you to rock the snowball back and forth with your tools, break it loose, and up it will go."

Okay, everybody, get ready," the Wizard said. They dug in with their picks and shovels and pushed hard as the balloon struggled to raise the snowball from the plain. "Now, Pickaplums, start rocking!"

The balloon hissed in desperation. It was rocking back and forth and almost busting at the seams. The Pickaplums grunted and groaned from the strain of pushing and pulling on their picks and shovels. Their faces turned beet red from the desperate struggle to free the giant snowball from the frozen plain. But try as they might, they could not rock the snowball loose. It seemed that the giant snowball was determined to keep Cloudine locked in its bowels forever.

"What do we do now, Wizard?" Princess Magenta asked.

By this time, Dee had fully recovered from the long pull and was very angry at the defiant snowball. "I'll show you what now! She screamed. "I worked too hard pulling the balloon over here, and I'm not going to let that overgrown, belligerent piece of ice keep Cloudine from us. Watch this."

While she talked, Dee was backing farther and farther away from the snowball. Then, with fire blazing from her nostrils, she started pawing the frozen plain, throwing ice over her hot, steaming body. She lowered her head and ran at the snowball like her seat was on fire. "Give us Cloudine!" she bellowed. Dee hit the snowball so hard that she drove her head to the bottom of the foot-deep ditch. Then she backed away and stood on wobbly legs. She almost knocked herself out! "Where am I? What day is this?" Dee asked.

The Pickaplums ran to Dee's side to keep her from falling over. "Are you okay, Dee?" Rosebud asked.

Before Dee could answer, they heard a strange noise coming from the snowball. It sounded like a squeaking, creaking door. The noise grew louder and louder, and then—

"Look at the snowball," Strawtop shouted. "It's splitting down the middle."

"Everyone run. Get out of the way or you'll be buried in the snow," shouted Mayor Tinge from his perch in the basket.

The Pickaplums ran from the huge splitting snowball, screaming, stumbling, and sliding on the frozen plain. When they turned to watch what was happening, they began to laugh and high five. At that moment the giant snowball gave what appeared to be a huge groan and split in half. It crumbled into two large piles of snow. Had the Pickaplums not gotten away in time, they would have been buried.

Princess Magenta and the Pickaplums were congratulating Dee for her heroics when the mayor called out, "I don't see Cloudine anywhere in the piles of snow. Maybe she disintegrated? What do we do now?" he asked.

CHAPTER XIX

WOULD HALF A CLOUDINE BE BETTER THAN NONE?

"Where's Cloudine? Does anybody see her?" The Pickaplums were crying and digging frantically for their missing friend.

"Pickaplums, please get off of the snow or you may accidentally crush Cloudine," Princess Magenta said. "The Wizard and I will search through the snow piles and see if we can uncover her. We'll call you when we find her, and then you can help."

The Wizard of Oz and the princess made their way cautiously up the huge piles of snow, shouting and probing for Cloudine.

"Shh. I think I hear a faint voice under me." The Wizard stopped and cupped his ears.

Princess Magenta moved across the pile of snow, bent over, and listened.

"Hello, Cloudine. Can you hear me?" the Wizard shouted at the pile of snow beneath his feet. A muffled voice replied.

"Did you hear that, Princess? It must be Cloudine!" the eager Wizard exclaimed.

"I heard it," the delighted princess said.

The two of them knelt down and gently dug into the pile of snow.

"Look, I've found a top hat," cried the thrilled Wizard.

They brushed away the snow around the top hat and were greeted by a big, warm Cloudine grin. "What took you so long to get here?" she joked.

Princess Magenta waved to the eager Pickaplums. "It's Cloudine! We found her! Come on up and help us dig her out."

"Isn't this a fine how do you do?" Cloudine said. "I feel rather foolish that I got caught up in the middle of a giant snowball. No more jumping over trees for me!"

"Are you okay, Cloudine?" Princess Magenta asked, patting her tenderly on the head.

"I don't know about the rest of me, because it's under the snow. But my head seems to be okay, and my brain and mouth are working." She laughed out loud.

"I need you children to use your hands and dig very carefully around and below Cloudine's head," the Wizard said. "See if you can uncover the rest of her body."

The children laughed and giggled with Cloudine as they dug away the snow. One of the children called out,

"She's definitely wrapped like a mummy in her long coat and scarf," and she placed the stocking cap on Cloudine's head.

Doctor Gottazaminya walked over to Cloudine and said, "I believe that your head is still attached to your shoulders. Move it around and see if it falls off." Cloudine moved her head around and around, and it stayed in place. "Your head seems to be okay, so it must be attached to your shoulders and arms." Doctor Gottazaminya told Cloudine, "Your upper limbs are okay. You can now move them freely."

Cloudine grabbed a shovel and started to dig herself out of the snow. Soon her fat body was released from the snow pile, allowing her freedom of movement.

"Hooray!" shouted the grining Cloudine. "At last I'm free from the giant snowball."

Cloudine pumped her arms into the air and reached out to hug the children, when suddenly, "Help me! My fat body has toppled over, and I'm starting to roll down the snow pile," she screamed. The children ran to Cloudine and stopped her from rolling. "We'll help you. We don't want you to become a snowball again," one of the children said.

"Oh no, my feet are gone!" Cloudine cried. "That's why I toppled over and started rolling. See if you can find my feet. They have my best pair of big black boots attached to them. Without my boots I can't walk. They are magic and hold my feet in place so they don't crumble." She chuckled anxiously. "Remember, children, I'm a snow woman, so you can always build me new feet. It's my boots that can't be replaced."

Everyone dug and dug but they couldn't find Cloudine's feet, or her magic black boots.

"You must hurry and find my boots. I have to entertain at a birthday party this evening," said Cloudine.

"Do you think that you lost your feet and boots on top of the mountain when you tripped over the log?" the princess asked.

"I may have," Cloudine said. "How can I possibly get to the top of the mountain to search for them without my feet and magic boots?"

"We don't have time to walk up the mountain and try to find them," the Wizard said.

"What can we do? We can't leave Cloudine here to freeze to the plain." Princess Magenta sobbed.

"There's only one way to save Cloudine, and that's with our balloon," the Wizard said. "She's too big for the basket, so we'll have to find a way to tie her to the bottom of it. Then we'll lift her up the side of the mountain, put her down by her home, find her feet and boots, and attach them to her."

"Sounds like a good plan to me," Strawtop said. "However, we can't tie her on with ropes. She's so heavy she'll fall apart before we can lift her off of the ground. We'll have to carry her in a sling. What can we use for a sling?"

"We have a large piece of canvas that we brought from the Teeny-taints' warehouse," Dee said.

The Wizard took charge. "Everyone, pitch in and let's make a sling. Grab the harness and ropes we used with Dee, spread them on the plain, and lay the canvas over the top of them."

When they had done as instructed, the Wizard said, "Now roll Cloudine onto the canvas, and everyone get into the basket and let's get her home."

Strawtop and Mayor Tinge tied the ropes to the bottom of the basket and handed two ropes to the Wizard. "You'll need these for ballast," Strawtop said.

"Princess Magenta, would you please ride with us to the top of the mountain?" the Wizard asked. "I need you to hold one of these ropes on one side of the basket while I hold the other on my side. Our weight will stabilize the load and keep Cloudine from swaying too much and falling out of the sling."

"With me in the basket, won't that be too much weight to lift?" Princess Magenta asked.

"I don't think so," the Wizard said. "Without her feet and boots, Cloudine's much lighter, so that will compensate for your extra weight in the basket. I can't bring you back to your village when we're finished because the prevailing wind will blow us too far away. So you'll have to walk home."

"The walk home will be good for me." Princess Magenta smiled at the Wizard. She stepped into the basket and grabbed the rope holding the sling. "Up we go, Wizard," she said.

The Wizard opened the valves and blasted hot air into the balloon. The balloon lifted off of the frozen plain, teetering ever so slightly.

"Whee! This is fun! I've never flown before, except as a few canteens full of water, and I don't remember that," Cloudine said. "Now, Wizard, take me to the top of the mountain, so I can entertain at the party tonight!

And whatever you do, please don't drop me." Cloudine was swinging and yodeling as up the imaginary elevator she rode.

"We won't drop you, Cloudine," the Wizard assured her. "But don't swing so far back and forth or you'll fall out of the sling. Then the children will be able to use you for a snowball fight."

Everyone laughed at the Wizard's joke.

"This is also my first flight, Cloudine, and I love it!" Princess Magenta said.

The balloon inched its way up the side of the mountain. Soon it was out of the shadows of the valley and into the setting sun. The hot air from the balloon and the hot blazing sun were taking their toll on Cloudine, and she was melting off several pounds.

"I'm losing so much water that I'm beginning to get weak. Better hurry," Cloudine urged.

"We're going up as fast as we can," the Wizard said. "Your weight is holding us down and causing the balloon to rise more slowly than we expected. But we'll get you home before you vanish, I promise. Now hang on tight."

A few minutes later, the balloon began to rise rapidly. This was because of the weight Cloudine was losing. They reached the top of the mountain, and flew over it before the Wizard could react. A north wind caught them, and they were swept away high over the shadowy frozen plain.

"Put me down! Put me down! I see my home!" Cloudine shouted.

There was nothing the Wizard could do. If he attempted to land, he had no idea how far from the mountain they would come down. Depending on where they landed, they might be killed, or seriously injured.

"Please put us down, Wizard. We can walk from here," Princess Magenta pleaded.

"You can't walk from here, Princess! Cloudine has no feet or magic boots! You'll have to go with us. I'll return you home after we find Kansas," the Wizard promised.

"Wizard, where did you say you are you going?" Cloudine asked.

"We're on our way to Kansas, Cloudine, a very large gray place. Have you ever seen Kansas from the mountaintops you've lived on?"

"I don't remember seeing Kansas," Cloudine said.

The balloon flew north, pushed by a steady breeze. Everyone wondered where they were, where they were going, or if this was the way to Kansas.

The Wizard thought: *What awaits us at the end of this frozen plain?*

CHAPTER XX

A DAZZLING LIGHT

The Wizard and his passengers flew steadily north for three days and nights without seeing Kansas or the end of the frozen plain. On the fourth day, the wind was at a standstill, and they were barely moving. To preserve fuel, the Wizard contemplated landing the balloon until the wind blew again. He knew that they would perish on the frozen plain if their fuel ran out. The Wizard informed everyone of the terrible situation they were in and said, "Unless there's one more miracle left for us, we're doomed."

"If only I didn't have this bad leg. Then I could fly out and locate a safe place for us," Dee shouted at the heavens.

"Hey, Dee, is that you?" a voice called out from above.

Everyone gazed around to see who had spoken to Dee. They feared it was another evil wizard.

"Yes, it's me!" Dee answered, doing a three-legged dance.

Immediately, a squadron of eight flying reindeer surrounded the basket. The reindeer were so happy to see Dee, that they were doing all kinds of acrobatic stunts, like loop-the-loops, flips, and figure eights. They were shouting and laughing. The leader of the squadron said, "Dee, at last we've found you!"

Dee laughed in disbelief. "Where did you come from, and how did you find me?"

The squadron leader hovered in front of Dee. "We've been all over the Alps for the last week, searching for you. Where have you been, and how did you get in that white basket?" Then he dropped down and stared in amazement at Cloudine hanging in the sling.

Dee told the reindeer of her own mishap with the balloon and the adventures that followed. Then she introduced everyone to her reindeer friends. Next, Dee explained who Cloudine was and how she had helped to lift her from the frozen plain. Continuing on, she said, "We're running out of fuel and supplies. Can you guys pull us off of this frozen plain so we can restock our supplies and head for a place called Kansas?"

"You bet we can!" the squadron leader replied. "That's what we're here for. Then he and the seven other flying reindeer each grabbed one of the eight mooring ropes in their teeth and pulled the balloon north toward a dazzling light. Everyone stared at the dazzling light and wondered why they hadn't noticed it until now. Was this another Shanevil trick?

The flying reindeer pulled the balloon north to the end of the great frozen plain. Ahead of them was a snow-covered mountain, rising high into the sky. The dazzling light was like a halo shining off the top of the mountain.

The reindeer towed the balloon into the center of the dazzling light, which was coming from a valley far below. Cloudine was hanging onto her sling, fearing for her life.

Terror gripped the Wizard and his crew. "I wonder, what awaits us in that valley below? Will we be safe there?"

"Perhaps Shanevil has found us and set a gruesome trap. He's going to destroy us," Rosebud cried.

CHAPTER XXI

A STARTLING DISCOVERY

The balloon, its passengers, and the eight flying reindeer were suspended momentarily in the dazzling light. Then the reindeer pulled the balloon downward. Soon they were below the dazzling light, and a wonderful panoramic scene was revealed.

"We're dropping down on a lush green valley surrounded by snow," Mayor Tinge said.

Dee was giggling at the sights. "The valley is filled with cool, clear mountain streams and lakes as blue as the summer sky," she said.

"I see trees laden with delicious fruits, and magnificent gardens overflowing with every kind of vegetable one could ever want," Princess Magenta cried.

"Look at that quaint village next to the bountiful orchards and gardens," Rosebud said.

Mayor Tinge was astonished by what he was seeing. "I can't believe how neatly this village is laid out with tree-lined streets, red brick sidewalks, and flower gardens in bloom."

"The village is full of gingerbread houses and shops. They're topped with roofs made of candies, marshmallows, and cotton candy, too," exclaimed Strawtop.

"Will you land us in the town square next to the gazebo?" the Wizard asked the reindeer.

The reindeer carefully pulled the balloon almost to the ground and stopped. They did not want to hurt Cloudine who was laughing with glee at the unbelievable sights.

Everyone climbed out of the basket and kissed the plush green grass surrounding the Town Square. The Wizard and his crew released Cloudine and rolled her under a cool, shady tree.

"I never thought we would see green grass again," Rosebud cried.

"I didn't either!" the princess agreed.

"Meow, meow," Apricot chimed in, scratching her back on a tree.

"I'm so happy to be here. If only I had my feet and boots, I would sing and dance for you!" Cloudine shouted. "It's amazing," she added. "It's hot in this shade and I'm not melting one bit. This is definitely a magical land."

A loud hiss was coming from the balloon. The fuel tanks had run dry, and the balloon had tipped over on its side. It lay on the ground with the last of the hot air hissing from it.

"Wow! That was close," the Wizard said. "If you reindeer hadn't brought us here when you did, we surely would have run out of fuel on the frozen plain and perished. By the way, squadron leader, how did you know to bring us here to this luscious green valley?"

"The Good Witch of the North told us to fly you here. She said that when we found you, we would see a dazzling light to the north. We were to pull the balloon to the light and bring it into this bright, booming valley."

"When you see the Good Witch of the North, please tell her we said thank you with all of our hearts," Mayor Tinge said.

No sooner had Mayor Tinge uttered these words, then the dazzling light that had been their guide began to grow smaller and smaller, until it was right next to them. The Good Witch of the North appeared in a flash, standing among them wearing a golden crown with her wand in hand.

"Tell me yourself, Mayor Tinge," the Good Witch of the North said with a smile. The Good Witch's golden hair and ruby red gown formed a dazzling light around her.

Rosebud spoke up. "Good Witch, are we in Kansas?"

"No, my dear child, you're in the North Pole. Kansas is far, far away. I must tell you that it wouldn't have done any good for you to go there. You see, Rosebud, you are what you are, just like everyone else. You were born to be short, and there is nothing you can do about it. However, you had the fortitude to try, and that's what's important. Because of your efforts, you are now in the North Pole with your new friends and Strawtop. Your new friends don't care what you look like, and I know you don't care what they look like either. I want each of you to know that if you are willing to stay here forever, and make the world happy, you'll always be happy too, not only now but for eternity."

I know we'll be happy here forever, and I want to stay that way," Rosebud said. She gave Strawtop's hand a squeeze. "You know, Good Witch, we almost didn't make it here. We could have been killed by lightning or from a crash in the Black Forest. We were almost buried in an avalanche, and almost perished on the frozen plain. How lucky we were to survive our frightening journey!"

"There wasn't a chance that anything bad would happen to you or anyone with you, my child," the Good Witch said. "You see, Dorothy told me of your trip to Kansas and your desire to become taller. She asked me to protect you and your friends on your journey.

"Rosebud, it was I who planted the idea in Dorothy's head to have you stow away in the pile of clothing. I was the one who brought Apricot to the basket, knowing how much she meant to you and that your happiness would be hollow without her.

"I visited you while you were sleeping under the pile of clothing, and placed a kiss on your left cheek. Anyone who saw the outline of the kiss could not harm you. You did not remember that I kissed you, and I did not want to tell you and take the element of danger out of your mission. Rosebud, I knew that the dangers you would face would make you feel like a much bigger person and give you the confidence you would need in life. I also knew that those who accompanied you would gain the same confidence, and they too would become better and stronger. And they have! I needed these traits in each of you, so you would be able to carry out a very special project here at the North Pole."

"What kind of special project?" Dee asked.

"It's my mission to make the children of the world happy for one day of the year. I have personally selected each of you for your many different talents. I also set up this North Pole village for you to do the work that needs to be done. From this day forward, each of you will be a part of my special project."

Strawtop said, "You, Good Witch of the North, have brought us safely to this beautiful village, and it would be my pleasure to work here. Helping make the children of the world happy would be very exciting. When can I get started?"

"First," said the Good Witch of the North, "if each of you likes the special project and the work I'm about to assign to you, you may stay here at the North Pole. However, if you don't like your assignment, you may pick another one, or you may return to your homes, with the exception of the Teeny-taints, of course. The avalanche caused by the wizard Shanevil destroyed their homes. And just so you'll know, it was I who freed the good wizard Shagoodie and trapped Shanevil inside the glass jug. I don't believe he will be bothering anyone ever again."

"How did you manage to trap Shanevil in the glass jug?" Mayor Tinge asked.

"I was watching the evil Shanevil through the fog, waiting for an opportunity to capture him and free the good wizard Shagoodie. When Shanevil threw the bolt of lightning that started the avalanche, he lost his balance and began to slide down the mountain. The only way he could escape the avalanche, and not be buried, was to shrink to the size of a snowflake and drift away. When Shanevil shrunk himself, I immediately caught him in the glass jug and popped the cork into it. And there he will stay forever, in the care of Shagoodie, unless someone takes out the cork and sets him free. Then, beware!"

Mayor Tinge and the Teeny-taints jumped up and down with glee.

"We'll do any special projects you want," Mayor Tinge said.

"What about our friends the Unkies? Where will they get their supplies without us making them?" Mayor Tinge asked.

The Good Witch gave Mayor Tinge a warm smile, "The reason I chose you to be one of my helpers was for your ability to see the problems of others. I know you'll make certain that the Unkies and millions of other people throughout the world will have the supplies they need, especially the children."

"Thank you for your confidence in me. What now?" the Wizard asked.

"I've kept you in the dark long enough. Here's what I want each of you to do," the Good Witch said, holding her magic wand above their heads.

CHAPTER XXII

SPECIAL ASSIGNMENTS ALL AROUND

The Good Witch of the North approached the Wizard of Oz with her magic wand held high, "Wizard of Oz you have always been a kindly man, one who imparts knowledge and confidence in everyone you meet. Once again, you have shown your bravery and wise decision making on this journey to the North Pole. You refused to give up the search for Kansas, even though Dorothy missed the trip. Once you found the stowaways on board, it was your intention to get to Kansas so Rosebud could grow taller. Though not a true wizard, you made others believe in themselves. Because of this, I'm making you a true wizard and the leader of this North Pole village."

After making her proclamation, the Good Witch touched the Wizard's head with her wand. Immediately, the Wizard's red suit, red hat, and red mittens—all with the white fur trim—his black boots and belt, and the red suspenders were transported from the white basket and placed upon him. The Wizard's white hair and beard grew longer, and he had a jolly "Ho, Ho, Ho," whenever he laughed.

"I know you were raised in Omaha, but where were you born?" the Good Witch asked.

"Reykjavik, Iceland."

"What is your real name?"

"My real name is Kris Kringle."

"Kris Kringle," the Good Witch proclaimed, holding her wand above his head, "from this day forward you shall be known as Santa Claus. It shall be your responsibility to oversee the making of toys, clothes, and other gifts for children around the world. It shall also be your responsibility to deliver these gifts as a part of my special project. Let it be known that from this day forward the gifts will be delivered on a very special day to be called, Christmas."

Santa Claus said, "Thank you for bestowing this great honor upon me. I shall do everything in my power not to disappoint you and to earn the trust you have placed in my ability. But tell me, Good Witch of the North, how will I deliver the gifts to the children on Christmas Day? As a true wizard, do I now have the ability to fly around the world and perform my job?"

"Yes, Santa Claus, being a true wizard, you do have the power to fly. However, this white balloon, which carried you to the North Pole, shall become your magical delivery sack. The balloon will start off the size of a backpack, and the more gifts you put in it, the bigger it will grow. This sack can grow large enough to hold the gifts for all of the children in the world. You can never fill this sack to the top, no matter how hard you try."

The Good Witch then touched the white balloon with her wand and shrunk it to the size of a backpack.

"How will I carry the sack full of presents? Won't it be too heavy for me?" Santa Claus asked.

"Santa Claus," the Good Witch said, "since you are now a true wizard, this sack can never be too heavy for you to carry. However, to make your delivery easier, I will supply you with a sleigh to carry you and your sack full of gifts."

The Good Witch walked over to the white basket and, touching it with her wand, transformed it into a gleaming red sleigh with gold runners and fancy gold decorations. A plush red leather seat for Santa Claus and a large cargo area for the sack full of gifts were added to the interior.

"This is wonderful," Santa Claus said. "Now that I'm a true wizard, I can grow some wings, use Dee's harness, and attach myself to the sleigh. Then I'll pull it around the world delivering the gifts to the children."

"You won't need to grow wings." The Good Witch smiled at him. "You can use the eight flying reindeer to pull your sled." She motioned for the reindeer to come to her. "You shall be the ones to pull Santa's sleigh. I name you, Dasher and Dancer, Prancer and Vixen, Comet and Cupid, Donner and Blitzen."

The Good Witch touched Dee's harness and the flying reindeer's antlers. In the blink of an eye, the flying reindeer were dressed in the finest of harnesses decorated with silver ornaments and golden, clanging, jingling bells. They pranced around with their heads held high, overjoyed to have such great responsibility. The eight white mooring ropes were transformed into black leather reins. "Santa Claus, these reins are for you to hang onto and guide your reindeer when you are making your deliveries."

Dee approached the Good Witch, limping noticeably. She had large reindeer tears in her eyes.

"I know I get lost a lot, but Good Witch, isn't there something I can do to help Santa Claus?"

"Dee," the Good Witch said, "it was your bravery that saved Cloudine. You drove yourself to exhaustion pulling the balloon across the frozen plain. Such bravery needs to be rewarded and, therefore, I have a very special assignment for you. I guarantee, when Santa Claus is delivering the gifts, no matter how bad the weather, it will be you who will never let him get lost!"

The Good Witch then healed Dee's injured leg with a touch of her wand. Dee could jump into the air and fly again. "Sometimes the Christmas nights will be too dark and foggy for Santa Claus to see where he's going. If Santa Claus should get lost, and not be able to deliver gifts to the good girls and boys, they would be terribly disappointed and stop believing in him. Therefore, I'm giving you a bright white nose with a radar system inside of it. With this magical nose, you and Rudolph will lead the other reindeer, and take Santa Claus on his appointed rounds. And when the deliveries are completed, you will be able to lead them back to the North Pole, no matter how bad the weather."

Dee knelt before the Good Witch to thank her. Touching Dee's nose with her wand, the Good Witch proclaimed, "Arise, Dee, and from this day forward, lead the way with Rudolph,"

Everyone was astounded to watch Dee's nose grow bigger and bigger, and whiter and brighter. Soon her nose looked like a bright spotlight on a fire truck.

"This is terrific! I love it!" She pranced around, making her nose blink on and off. "Even better, you can call me Dee, the White Nosed Reindeer."

"Where will we possibly get enough toys, clothes, and foods to fill this sack for Christmas Day?" Santa Claus wanted to know.

The Good Witch said, "I'm turning the Teeny-taints into elves. They will be dressed alike so that none of them will be less or more important than anyone else. They will wear candy-striped, pointed stocking caps. Each hat will have a red and white ball on the top. The Teeny-taints will also wear green jackets and pants with a gold rope belt tied around the middle. Each of their jacket collars will be red, and their pointy-toed, green boots will have a silver bell on top.

"It will be the elves' responsibility to make the toys, clothes, and other items for the children of the world, like they did for the Unkies. You elves will have everything ready for Santa Claus to deliver by Christmas Eve." The Good Witch then placed her magic wand above the Teeny-taints' heads, and turned them into elves, dressed in elves' clothing.

"This is wonderful! We can make our favorite things forever!" Mayor Tinge said. "You can count on us to have everything put in Santa's sack and loaded on the sleigh whenever he's ready to go!"

"No. Loading the gifts onto Santa's sleigh will not be your job," the Good Witch replied. "You elves are only to make the presents. Rosebud and Strawtop are bigger and stronger than the rest of you, so it will be their responsibility to load the sleigh for Christmas Day delivery." The Good Witch touched Rosebud and Strawtop with her wand, and the two of them were dressed exactly like the other elves.

Rosebud, Strawtop, and their fellow elves held hands and danced in a circle, delighted with their new responsibilities.

A loud shout came from under the tree.

"Hey, Good Witch of the North, what about me?"

It was Cloudine. She had been forgotten during the excitement.

"Is there anything you can do for Cloudine?" Santa Claus asked.

"Yes indeed!" the Good Witch replied. "Cloudine," she said, "you have entertained others and taken care of the children in the Alps for years. I'm making it your responsibility to entertain, not only the children of the North Pole, but the children of the world.

"Cloudine the snow woman, it will be your job to baby-sit for the children of the North Pole while their parents are working. You'll lead the children on parades down the streets of town and have fun playing many kinds of games. You'll also do the same thing for children throughout the world. Whenever it snows, you shall be there making them happy."

With a touch of her wand, the Good Witch gave Cloudine two new feet with new big, black, shiny magic boots on them

Cloudine jumped to her new feet and began parading and singing. She would be a great entertainer again.

Cloudine gave out a, "Whee!" She began sliding down the snow banks that surrounded the village.

"And now for you, Princess Magenta," the Good Witch said. "You and Santa Claus belong together. You have professed your love for each other. Do you love Santa Claus?"

"Yes, I do!" the princess said with a blush.

"And you, Santa Claus, do you love the princess?"

"With my whole heart," Santa Claus replied.

"Then by the powers invested in me, I pronounce you Mr. and Mrs. Santa Claus. Mrs. Claus, it will be your duty to make cookies, cakes, pies, candies, and other goodies just as you did when you were a princess. Santa Claus will deliver them to the children of the world."

"Thank you for this wonderful assignment and for making me Mrs. Santa Claus," Princess Magenta said with a curtsy.

Everyone began to chant, "Thank you. Thank you," over and over again. But someone was heard sobbing in the background.

"Who is that crying?" the Good Witch asked.

CHAPTER XXIII

A HAPPY CONCLUSION

The eight flying reindeer and Dee had gone to their new pasture and barn to relax and eat some hay and oats. They were grateful to have Dee and her bright white nose with them because she could light up the barn when it got dark.

Mayor Tinge had assembled the elves and told them to pick out a house. "We have a lot of work to do tomorrow," he said. "So everyone get to bed early, and whatever you do, don't take the big house next to the Town Hall. That one belongs to Mr. and Mrs. Santa Claus."

Cloudine the Snow woman was running around the streets of town and into the woods, picking out trails to parade on so she could keep the children occupied when she babysat them.

Meanwhile, Rosebud was weeping softly.

The Good Witch saw this and said, "Rosebud, was it you I heard sobbing when everyone was thanking me? Why are you crying now? You have been a delight to watch. You faced the many challenges I gave to you during these past few weeks. It's wonderful that you and Strawtop found each other. I know that the two of you will forever be happy together."

"That's all well and fine," said Rosebud, "and I do appreciate how pleased you are with me. I'm certainly happy with Strawtop, happier than I've ever been in my whole life. In fact, as long as we are together here on the North Pole, I won't ever wish to be taller again. It's my mother and father that I'm worried about. I told them that I would come home when I got taller, and now I don't have any way to get there. Will I ever see them again?" Rosebud asked, wiping away a tear.

"Of course you will," the Good Witch said. "Watch!" and with that, she touched the ground with her magic wand. "Poof," there standing in front of Rosebud was Mama Bellpepper and Papa Parsleysprig.

Rosebud embraced her mama and papa. She told them where they were and what had happened to her over the past few weeks.

"You've been brought here at Rosebud's request," the Good Witch told Mama Bellpepper and Papa Parsleysprig. "If you wish to stay in the North Pole, you must take an assignment and work on it while you are here."

"What do you want them to do?" Rosebud asked.

"Every year, Santa Claus will get letters from children around the world, telling him what they want for Christmas. Papa, since you're an accountant, and because you like to work with figures, it will be your task to assemble a list of what each child wants. You'll give the list to the elves, and they'll manufacture the requests. When the elves are finished, you'll provide a delivery list for Rosebud and Strawtop, and they will load everything onto Santa's sleigh in the correct order of delivery. What do you think of this most important job?" the Good Witch asked.

"I'll do it! I can't think of any job that I would enjoy more," Papa Parsleysprig replied with a big, satisfied grin.

The Good Witch turned to Mama Bellpepper and said, "You are a wonderful cook and pastry maker. I would like you to work with Mrs. Claus helping her make the goodies for Christmas Day and throughout the rest of the year. Do you think you would like this assignment, and will it make you happy?"

"I think that this assignment will make me the happiest person in the North Pole," Mama Bellpepper said.

Rosebud was beaming like a beacon in the night, as she, Mama Bellpepper, Papa Parsleysprig, and Apricot walked to their new home. They had so much to talk about.

"Everything has worked out fine, Good Witch," Santa Claus said. "It will be interesting to see what happens when we have our first Christmas Day delivery."

"You'll do a great job with your first delivery and every one thereafter." The Good Witch smiled. "It's important to remember that when you deliver presents to each of the homes, not every one will have a chimney for you to climb down. If they don't, you can go through the front or back doors of the houses, or through cracks in the floors or walls. Being a true wizard means that you can make the sack and yourself bigger or smaller in order to deliver the gifts. You must make every delivery at any cost!"

"I will, and I promise you, no child on my list will be without a gift on Christmas Day." Santa gave a hearty "Ho, Ho, Ho!"

"I must go now," the Good Witch said. "I have much work to do. If you need me, just call. No matter where I am, I'll hear you."

"Goodbye, Good Witch. You are truly the bearer of good will and sunshine."

"I have passed those honors to you, Santa Claus," said the Good Witch of the North. Then she placed a warm, red kiss on Santa's nose and cheeks and disappeared in a flash of light.

Santa Claus's nose and cheeks turned cherry red when the kisses from the Good Witch of the North were placed upon them. They remain that way to this very day.